Short Stories
of To-day and Yesterday

GERALD BULLETT

SHORT STORIES *of* TO-DAY & YESTERDAY

First Volumes

ARNOLD BENNETT
W. W. JACOBS
GEORGE GISSING
A. NEIL LYONS
GUY DE MAUPASSANT
ANTHONY TROLLOPE
BRET HARTE
BARRY PAIN
ARTHUR MORRISON
MORLEY ROBERTS
G. K. CHESTERTON
EDEN PHILLPOTTS
ERNEST BRAMAH
GERALD BULLETT
IRVIN S. COBB

Short Stories
of To-day and Yesterday

GERALD
BULLETT

GEORGE G. HARRAP *&* CO. LTD.
LONDON   BOMBAY   SYDNEY

First published 1929
by GEORGE G. HARRAP & CO. LTD.
*39-41 Parker Street, Kingsway, London, W.C.*2

Printed in Great Britain by William Brendon & Son, Ltd.
The Mayflower Press, Plymouth

INTRODUCTORY NOTE

*T*HOSE *who are inclined to be dubious about the present state of the short story in England would do well to take note of Gerald Bullett. Here is a writer who can spin a yarn briskly and neatly—the first requisite for the short-story-teller—but one also who can do much more than that. Gerald Bullett has the understanding which realizes that the things which fill our normal vision are but superficial, and that the commonplace is often the vesture of the wildly fantastic. The most ordinary appearances may cloak the grimmest tragedy, and the uncanny often lurks round the most unpromising corner. A little girl in one of his stories gazes out of the window to see " the hugest dog in the world . . . staring with the most sinister intention straight up at her." She shrinks back in deadly fear, but finds on closer scrutiny that it is only a bush after all. We are all more or less like that. The things we see are ever changing, and we can never be sure we are looking at a perfectly harmless bush or a terribly ferocious dog. This is the burden of Mr Bullett's tales. The amiable farmer who is acting as host becomes a fiendish monster. The benevolent uncle develops into an ogre. A casual client reawakens and embodies a past long dead. A very little separates the most prosaic person among us from the bizarre and the inexplicable. We are always trembling on the brink of wild tragedy.*

And closely allied to Mr Bullett's gift for conveying this sense of the underlying mystery of things is his keen eye for a contrast. Here is an example: "So sequestered is the little valley in which I have made my solitary home that I never go to town without the delicious sensation of poising my hand over a lucky-bag full of old memories." That is neatly and delicately expressed, and the neatness and delicacy are typical of Mr Bullett's work.

Gerald Bullett was born in 1894 and was educated at Cambridge. Besides volumes of short stories, he has written novels, tales of adventure, and critical studies. To the series entitled "These Diversions" he very appropriately contributed a volume on "Dreaming."

Thanks are due to Messrs John Lane The Bodley Head, Ltd., for permission to reprint "The Baker's Cart," "Simpson's Funeral," "The Bending Sickle," "Summers End," "The Sunflowers," and "Prentice," from "The Baker's Cart"; "The Street of the Eye," "Sleeping Beauty," "The Mole," "Miss Lettice," and "Dearth's Farm," from "The Street of the Eye"; and to Messrs William Heinemann, Ltd., for "The Grasshopper," "The Puritan," and "The World in Bud," from "The World in Bud."

F. H. P.

CONTENTS

CONTENTS

7

THE MOLE

CONVERSATION turned inevitably to the local tragedy that was agitating all the village. The little general store, the only shop the place boasted and a poor thing at that, had been burned down in the night, and nothing remained but the heap of ruins from which, not many hours since, two charred corpses had been removed. Our chessmen stood in battle array, ready for action, but unnoticed by either of us. Something in Saunders's manner held my attention. Sceptic though I am, I have always found him interesting. He pays me the compliment of divesting himself of his rectorship when he visits me, and it has flattered my vanity to believe that I see a side of him that is for ever hidden from those of his parishioners who assemble Sunday by Sunday to receive from him their spiritual ration. And I was the more attracted because I divined depths in him still to be explored.

Perhaps I am over-fanciful (said Saunders, edging his chair nearer to the fire); but it had always seemed to me that there was more in their marriage than the mere female domination so obvious to everyone. And when poor Gubbins came to me last winter, with the story that I'm going to tell you, my guess was confirmed. Mrs Gubbins wore the breeches—a vulgar phrase for a vulgar thing—but that wasn't all. I shall never forget my first visit to her shop. You've seen the woman scores of times, but I'll tell you the impression she made on me. Her face was leather ; her nose was pinched and pitiless ; her eyes—did you ever notice her eyes ? You'd expect her to possess the malignant dominating eyes of the shrew. No such thing. Mrs Gubbins's eyes resembled those of a mask, or of a corpse : they were fixed, so it seemed to me, in a cold, everlasting, fishy scrutiny of a drab world. If they were the windows of her soul, they were windows made of frosted glass. Looking at them I seemed to see vacuity behind them. Looking again, I surmised a soul indeed, but a damned soul. A professional prejudice, perhaps, that you won't sympathize with. But it was not her eyes that most disturbed me. I have seen a variety of unpleasant eyes. But I have never seen on any human being so ugly a mole as was on that woman's chin. It was about the size of a pea, and growing from it were three longish black whiskers. The thing looked positively feline. It became for me, as soon as I caught sight of it, her most significant feature. And that, too, proved a good guess.

I had gone to the shop ostensibly to buy a cake of soap, but really in the hope of catching a glimpse of a human soul, of two human souls.

I had heard queer accounts of this couple, and I was curious.

"A cake of soap, please, Mrs Gubbins." I was then a stranger to her, as to all the village, but my use of her name evoked no sign of life in those glassy eyes of hers. She turned to her husband, that mild little man with dreaming eyes and a trim beard who looked just what he was, a lay preacher with a taste for fantastic prophecy. He was sitting at the back of the shop on a case of sugar, or something of the kind, engrossed in reading his pocket Bible.

"Run along," said Mrs Gubbins, in her flat, expressionless voice. "Soap, George! You know where it is!"

The little man looked up with the air of one dragged unwillingly from a dream. In his small rabbit-eyes Christian patience did battle with resentment. I seemed to scent a crisis. Had the woman nagged him for his idleness I couldn't have blamed her. But what interested me was not the rights and wrongs of the quarrel, but its method.

He blinked at her defiantly. There was a pregnant silence during which they stared at each other. Then the woman, protruding her chin, elongating her thin neck, bent a little towards him. I was dumbfounded with astonishment and a kind of morbid curiosity. For the moment it seemed to me that she must be mutely demanding a kiss in token of his submission; but while I watched, fascinated out of

11

my good manners, she lifted her hand slowly and placed her index finger upon the point of her chin. It flashed on me that she was directing his attention to that mole of hers.

Gubbins averted his eyes and slid off the seat. " Yes, dear ! " he muttered, and disappeared into the bowels of the shop.

II

Secrets of the confessional ? Yes, in a sense. But Gubbins wouldn't grudge you the story now. It was during that phenomenally cold spell in November, fifteen months ago, that he came to me. That he came to me at all should tell you something of his anguish of spirit, if you knew the man. Everybody knew him to be a deeply religious person, of the Bible-punching kind, but not everybody guessed how his particular conception of reality had eaten into his mind. He could prove to you by an elaborate system of Scriptural cross-references that the Day of Judgment was due to occur in the summer of 1950 ; and the geography of heaven was more familiar to him, and more concrete, than the chairs and tables in his own house or the streets of this village. Two-thirds of him lived among these precise, humourless dreams of his, dreams that were the fruit not of mystical experience, but of a laborious investigation, with rule and compass and a table of logarithms, extended over fifteen years. Two-thirds of him—that means he was more than a little unbalanced. He was a preposterous combination of arrogance and humility: we had many a friendly argument together, though the friendliness, I fancy, was rather on my side. Blandly certain of being the custodian of divine truth, he was yet pitifully dubious about his own chance of salvation and almost crazy in his forlorn pursuit of the love of God. Almost, but not quite: in the medical sense he was undoubtedly as sane as you or I. Me and all my kind he disliked because we receive payment for preaching Christ. That is what makes his appeal to me so remarkable an event.

Well, he came to the Rectory and was admitted by the maid, loyal to her orders to exclude no one, but scared. I found him standing on my study hearthrug, his face ashen, his lean, hairy hands clutching a cloth cap as though it were his only hold on safety. The white knuckles gleamed like polished ivory. I saw the fear that flared in his tiny eyes and guessed that he had come as a suppliant, that in some way his faith in himself was broken. And knowing of old the obstinate strength of that faith, I shuddered.

" In trouble, Mr Gubbins ? "

He appeared not to see my outstretched hand. " I've had an escape from hell," he squeaked. " It's that damned monkey-spot, Mr Saunders."

The mild expletive, coming from Gubbins, astonished me no less than his statement. I asked him to sit down and tell me all about it, but he remained standing, and his fingers twitched so violently that presently his cap fell to the ground unheeded. "It nearly got me, sir, that monkey-spot." A local expression, no doubt; but what did it mean? Gubbins saw at last that I didn't understand him. "That monkey-spot on her chin. My wife's chin. You must have seen it."

Can you imagine two human beings, tied by marriage, devoting all their emotional energy to hating each other? Perhaps not; but that is, as near as I can tell it to you, the truth about the Gubbinses. Twenty years ago she was an unremarkable woman, and he, no doubt, a very ordinary youth. Mere propinquity, I imagine, threw them at each other. He, with little or nothing of the genuine affection that might have excused the act, took advantage of her, as the phrase is. Sin number one, the first link in the chain that was to bind him, the first grievance for her to cherish in her ungenerous heart. They were married three months before the birth of the child. It died within an hour. She chose to see in this event the punishment of the sin into which he, as she contended, had betrayed her. From that moment Gubbins was her thrall: not by virtue of love, or the legal tie, but by virtue of the hideous moral ascendancy that the woman had been cunning enough, and pitiless enough, to establish over him. Carefully she kept alive the memory of his offence. It was a whip ready to her hand. And when seeking for distraction from his domestic misery he turned to that intricate game of guesswork which was for him religion, what he learned there of the significance of sin only served to increase his wretchedness.

He was evidently a man weak both in spirit and intelligence, or he would have realized at once that he was no more guilty than she was. But once she had succeeded in imposing her view upon him he could not shake it off. It remained, to poison his self-respect. Side by side with his conviction of unworthiness there grew up a hatred of the woman he was supposed to have wronged. And, being itself sinful, this very hatred provided a further occasion for remorse. It was a race between loathing and repentance, and loathing won. Never a personable woman, Mrs Gubbins became daily more repellent, until at last the wretched husband found her mere presence a discomfort, like an ill-fitting shoe or a bad smell. In particular, he detested—as well he might—that mole on her chin with its three feline hairs. And she, fiendishly acute, found it all out. She caught his sidelong glances of distaste, and pondered them long; and that distaste became another weapon to her hand. She accused him of harbouring cruel thoughts; taunted him with first robbing her of youth and then despising her for lacking it; flung out wild and baseless charges of infidelity. To propitiate her he made the most fantastic concessions: allowed her to turn him out of the shop, and consented to do all the housework in her stead. It became patent to the world that she was master.

You'll ask why he was fool enough to put up with this treatment? But, given his weakness, the explanation is credible enough. She attacked him at his most vulnerable point, his conscience. Religion, as he conceived it, taught him to submit to circumstances, not to master them. In his darkest hour he could still kneel at his bedside and say, " Thy will, not mine, be done." And he really believed for a while that God's will and Mrs Gubbins's were in mystical accord, that she, in fine, was the rod with which, for his own soul's good, heaven was scourging him. To aid this grotesque delusion there was the spectacle of her formal piety. For she was a prayerful woman, scrupulous in her speech, and of unquestioned honesty in her commercial transactions.

If only he could have cursed her and stood by his words, she might have mended. But he, who believed he had unravelled the ultimate secrets of destiny, dared not pit his moral judgment against hers. He was ever ready to sit on the stool of repentance. A day came when hatred rose to a frenzy in him. He cut short her complaints with an oath, poured out the gall of his heart upon her. She seemed quelled, and in his triumph he added a taunt, banal and, indeed, puerile : " You whiskered old cat ! " It was a fatal mistake. She stared at him mutely for a moment, no doubt in sheer astonishment.

Then her eyes narrowed and something like a smile twisted her lips. " Cat and mouse," she remarked coldly. And—call the man a fool, if you like—that reply terrified Gubbins as nothing else could have done.

He had betrayed himself once more into the hands of the enemy. He had provided her with a new and a bitter grievance. Worst of all, she knew his secret, knew that his loathing centred on that monkey-spot of hers, as he called it. From that moment I imagine her cherishing that mole with the solicitude that Samson, had he been a wiser man, would have lavished upon his hair. It was the source and the instrument of her power. So far as I understood Gubbins, it was as much nausea as hatred that the thing inspired in him. His soul sickened at the sight of it. It became a poison, a torture. All this she knew and exulted in. . . . Curious that an æsthetic sense, together with a weak stomach, should suffice to work a man's downfall.

And so I come back to that night of fear the events of which drove Gubbins, twenty hours later, but still electric with terror, to the refuge of my study.

III

Saunders paused to relight his pipe. One disconcerting thing about the affair (he resumed after a while) is that in Gubbins's account of his wife I can discover no human qualities at all. I fancy he himself had begun to regard her as an agent, not of God this time, but of the devil. Characteristic of him to jump from one pole to the other. And that theological fantasia, his imagination, may have coloured everything. That is as it may be. I can only tell you what he told me.

You know how quickly some noxious weed will overrun a flower-bed. Well, something of the kind happened in the ill-disciplined mind of Gubbins. He was pitifully susceptible to suggestion. An idle fancy presented itself to him : " Many a woman has been murdered for less than that monkey-spot." And the fancy became a fear which walked with him night and day, a fear lest he should be betrayed by sheer force of suggestion into murdering his wife. You realize what that would mean : it would mean damnation for his soul, or so he believed. The gallows had but few terrors for him. I think he would have welcomed death, could he have been sure of his salvation hereafter.

The seed was sown. The idea took root. And the more passionately he struggled against it, the more persistently his imagination envisaged the crime. At last one night, after a hundred sleepless hours, he reached the end of his tether.

He jumped noiselessly out of bed. Moonlight flooded the room, imparting a ghastly pallor to the face of the supine Mrs Gubbins. In sleep she had something of the chill dignity of a corpse lying in state. The thin lips curled back a little on one side of the mouth, and in the gap gleamed a gold-crowned tooth, a tiny yellow fang. On the point of her chin was that at which the wretched man tried not to look : itself not very offensive, but rendered hideous by the three black, jealously guarded hairs depending from it. Gubbins swears that as he stood staring at his wife's face those hairs were moving to and fro like the long legs of a spider, or the antennæ of an insect seeking prey.

Having gazed long, he forced his fascinated eyes away, and padded across the room. The door clicked, in spite of him, as he opened it. He experienced all the alarms of a guilty man. Yet his intention was innocent enough : it was even, in its grotesque fashion, comical. He had resolved to shear this female Samson of her power by cutting off those three hairs.

But when he returned to the bedside, and stood again by the sleeping body of his wife, he was overcome by nausea. Distaste for the task paralysed his will. He felt as a sensitive man would feel if he were forced to crush a beetle with his naked finger. As an excuse for delay he began examining the instrument in his hand, which was a perfectly ordinary pair of household scissors, having, as all scissors have, one sharp end and one blunted. The sharp end interested him most. He scrutinized its point and pressed it against the ball of his thumb ; and the thought flashed to him, as though the devil himself had whispered it : " This is sharp enough—one thrust under the left ear." He shuddered, recoiled from the idea, and burned with shame and fear for having ever had it. And, while still suffocating with the sense of his own guiltiness, there crept into his consciousness the nightmare conviction that he was being watched. He could not see his wife, his gaze being fixed on the scissors, but he knew that she had opened her eyes.

Gubbins couldn't explain to me the horror of that moment. He merely bowed his head on my mantelpiece and closed his eyes as if to shut out an evil vision. For when, after an age of immobility and silence, he forced himself to look at the face on the bed, he saw the cruel lips curled in a smile of final triumph; and even the opaque eyes seemed for once to shine. And what, for Gubbins, gave the last turn to the screw of terror was that the woman was not looking at him at all. Her gaze, full of evil beatitude, was fixed on the ceiling. For several minutes, minutes that throbbed with his agony, she neither moved nor spoke; and at last, very slowly, she moved a little higher on to the pillow and, still smiling insanely, bared her throat for him to strike. Gubbins was convinced that she ardently desired him to stain his soul with her blood.

Well, as you know, he didn't murder her: not that time, at any rate. He escaped, as he said, from hell. But I think I would as soon go to hell as have to live through those last fifteen months of his. For now she had completed his enslavement; now she had got his miserable little soul between her finger and thumb. Added to all her old grievances, those daggers with which to stab at his conscience, she had another and a more sensational one : this terrible sin, this attempt upon her life. Spiritual blackmail prolonged for twenty years. No wonder he set fire to the place.

From " The Street of the Eve "

THE BENDING SICKLE

Young Corbett returned from lunch just in time to open the door of his bank for a crooked old lady who appeared too feeble, or too timid, to effect an entry without aid. Her white wisps of hair straying from under a queer little bonnet, and the parchment pallor of her wrinkled skin, contrasted so oddly with the innocent blue of the eyes she turned towards him that for a brief moment the boy's heart faltered in the presence of unnamable premonition. There was a touch of gallantry, as well as of proprietorship, in the gesture with which, having ushered her in, he bestowed on her the freedom of the institution from which he received twenty-five shillings a week.

The old lady, leaning on her ebony stick, approached the bank counter with an air of profound resolution, and in a low voice made known her wishes to the cashier. Could she see the manager?

"I will see if he is disengaged," said the cashier. "What name may I say?"

"Eh?" She had failed to hear. "I want him to take care of something for me."

"Certainly. May I send in your name?"

She shook her head, and smiled wistfully.

" No, I haven't got it with me. It's in the taxi outside. Perhaps someone would be kind enough to carry it in for me. It's rather heavy, don't you see."

The cashier seemed embarrassed.

" Perhaps that nice young man who opened the door for me . . . if he would be so good. A black tin box, but rather heavy, you know."

Young Corbett was summoned, and dispatched on this errand ; and the cashier addressed himself once again to the task of discovering his client's name. Having at last succeeded, he did his best to look as though he had known it all the time.

" Of course ! How forgetful of me ! " he exclaimed, although he had in fact never seen this lady before. " I'm afraid the manager is out at the moment, Mrs Severn. Perhaps you would like a word with our Mr Turner ? "

Our Mr Turner had to be approached with some caution. He was a bald, kindly, obstinate old man, permanently embittered by the knowledge that he was an anachronism, a professional failure, fifteen years older than the manager under whom he worked.

" A Mrs Severn wants to see you, sir."

Mr Turner turned a cold eye on the spoiler of his peace, and slightly shifted his position on the tall stool, across the back of which his long black coat-tails hung in rigid propriety. " Where's the manager ? "

" Out, sir."

23

With extreme reluctance Mr Turner laid down his pen, adjusted his pince-nez, and rose.

In the manager's room he found Mrs Severn already seated. He became at once the embodiment of polite urbanity. The bank would be delighted to be of service to Mrs Severn. The deed-box should be deposited in the safe, and a receipt issued. Had Mrs Severn an account here? No? Ah, yes, the late Mr Severn had had an account. Of course. He remembered it perfectly.

He pressed a bell-push on the manager's desk. Corbett answered the ring.

"Make out a safe-custody receipt for this box, contents unknown. The name is Mrs Severn. Let me see, have we your full name, Mrs Severn?"

"Cathleen," said the old lady, when at last the question reached her. "Cathleen Severn."

"Thank you," said Corbett, bowing, and went back into the outer office.

While they waited, the bank official and the client, for the return of Corbett with the receipt ready for signature, Mr Turner sat in pensive silence. Conversation with this lady was too difficult a matter; and, indeed, he himself was rather hard of hearing. He allowed his thoughts to wander. Cathleen. How incongruously the name had sounded on the old lady's lips. Well, not so old, perhaps, but oldish, oldish—like himself. Mr Turner was vaguely aware that Cathleen was a name which had once held some special significance for him. He could distinctly remember how, in his youth, he had never seen or heard it without an echo of an old emotion. He recalled the echo; he recalled vaguely the emotion; but whatever had first occasioned that emotion now eluded him.

II

Michael Antony Turner was twenty-one, a bank-clerk on holiday. Already he had spent three days of his fortnight's leave, and spent them very profitably, as he considered: solitary, cooking and cleaning for himself, in a two-roomed cottage in Little Essex situated on the left of the High Street where it bends round the lower pool past the old market-place, now disused. Much of his time, and all his thought, had been given not to these domestic affairs but to self-perfection in the process of making woodcuts. He had brought with him, besides the homespun suit he stood up in, three extra shirts, five pairs of socks, two toothbrushes, a comb, and shaving tackle. All these he had stowed into a haversack, too new to be picturesque, of which he had been intermittently conscious all the while it had lain in the rack of the railway carriage. He would have walked the long distance cheerfully; indeed he would have delighted to walk, exulting in sore heels and the adventure of sleeping in the lee of haystacks and waking with farmyard smells in his nostrils. He was very much in earnest, very innocent of affectation : a creature still dewy with youth.

He stood in the post office, absently fingering a little oblong of thin paper which the girl at the counter had given him in exchange for a parcel. A self-conscious impulse made him look up. In the girl's eyes the ghost of a surprised kindliness still lingered ; maternal amusement hovered about her mouth and slightly dimpled her cheek.

Michael's glance rested upon her with satisfaction. And while he stared, something unprecedented happened to him. She was tall, built on a generous scale, yet gracefully and perfectly proportioned. He noticed, with a curious spasm of surprise, her broad brow, the full and kindly contours of her face, the unique charm of blue eyes and dark hair. Where had he seen her before ? He had never seen her before. Yet he felt this meeting to be at once an adventure and a home-coming ; he felt as an exile may feel when at a turn of the lonely road he comes upon some vision of meadow and sky that is intimate and dear, yet strange.

He blushed to find himself staring. " Oh, and may I have a dozen stamps ? "

She smiled. Summer lightning played over her features, a tiny lyric of laughter too frail for sound. " You may, surely. Is it any particular kind you're wanting ? "

When he had received his stamps and paid for them, they exchanged good morning, and he went out into the spring sunlight. The street was transfigured. Even the red letter-box, let into the post office wall, had become an apocalypse of beauty. Back went Michael to his cottage, a three miles' walk along country roads. His body moved on in a world that had the perfection of a work of art, but his mind remained exquisitely poised, contemplating the burning beauty whose limbs this visible creation did but transparently veil. "Life of life . . ." He recited two stanzas of Shelley to the heedless hedges.

As he turned into the High Street of his village, he dodged across the road to avoid his loquacious landlord, old George Proudfoot. George was the most sensational feature of Little Essex. He resembled nothing so much as a blasphemous parody of God the Father. He was white-haired, saintly in appearance, and nearly always drunk. His obscene jests were the pride of three local taverns. But to-day Michael was in no mood for George.

He entered the cottage, lunched off bread and cheese, and dreamed his day away. Seven o'clock, closing time, found him back in the little provincial town again, hovering near the post office in hope of seeing her. But when at last she emerged she was accompanied by a friend, a dumpy girl, a parody of humankind. Michael, shamefaced but desperate, followed the two at a respectful distance through several streets, until a little grey villa engulfed them both.

The days of his leave sped on into the void, never to be recovered. That is how he himself thought of it. And then, with all the unexpectedness of crisis, he saw her again. With her dumpy friend she was entering a field where local sports were to be held. The place was gay with bunting, which floated, like the pennons of ships, over a sea of chatter and perspiration.

The two girls took up their stand on the outskirts of the crowd. There was a clear path to her. A sack-race was beginning. Michael had lived for twenty-one years without ever discovering before the consuming interest that a sack-race held for him. He expiated this neglect in an instant's enthusiasm.

He was at her side, raising his hat, blushing and murmuring. She acknowledged his existence coldly. The attendant goblin scowled. Then, with mutterings and furtive gestures, it began to scold. Michael's heart threatened to leap out of his body. Would these insulted young women call a policeman? But the mutterings and furtive gestures produced no visible effect in the face of deity.

Said Michael, reciting his rehearsed part :

" I wrote a letter to you yesterday."

" Did you, then ? " Deity appeared amused.

" I haven't seen it."

" No. I didn't post it. I couldn't, not knowing your name. I was on the way to the post office to deliver it by hand, when I saw you going into the enclosure here."

She hesitated before asking : " And the letter —what was it all about ? "

" It was an apology."

" Indeed ? "

" Yes. It's very kind of you to pretend not to understand. It was disgraceful of me to follow you about the other night, quite unpardonable. But I couldn't help it."

" Oh, that ! " she said. " I was awfully sorry about that. I'd no idea you meant to wait for me. It took me by surprise."

He swam in a sea of delicious implications.

III

From that to the ultimate avowal was an inevitable step. They had walks and talks together, and at last, one day, after a morning's work, she was able to give him nine consecutive hours of her intoxicating company. The day was radiant. They walked in a world of flame. To Michael it was as if she moved, a queen of beauty, amid the loveliness that she herself had created. He was extravagant, and he recognized his extravagance. He had never felt so idiotic and so happy. He felt himself to be alone with Cathleen in a beautiful, unreal universe. Only themselves, and his love for her, were real.

Their road led to a bridge that ran over a railway cutting. They climbed a gate and sat down, side by side, on the green dry turf of the embankment. The road arched over them. All things conspired to urge that this, and no other, was the supreme moment, the pivot upon which the whole world turned.

"I've got something to say," he faltered.

"Yes."

"And I'm dreadfully afraid, because, you see, I don't believe the things you believe, and . . ."

"You mean you're a Protestant," she helped him out.

"No. I simply don't believe, that's all. I can't. And the terrible thing is . . ." He lost command of his voice. His heart beat dangerously. His face flamed.

She suddenly had hold of his hand and was caressing it with her own. "Yes, I know," she said soothingly, as to a little child.

"You see," he went on, on the verge of tears, "I'm so dreadfully in love with you."

He had said it, and now she must answer him. The pause was an agony, but a beautiful agony.

"If only you were my religion," she said.

He looked up. "What did you say?"

"I wish you were a Catholic, like me, Michael."

"You mean . . . ?"

"I couldn't marry any but a Catholic."

He stared into his lap again and sighed. "I thought so."

"It isn't that I'm not very fond of you," she said.

30

What angel from heaven could have said more? He turned, put his arm about her, and drew her towards him. Just as he was going to kiss her she turned away her head. Their eyes met.

"Mustn't I?"

She shook her head, but her eyes were tender.

"No. I'd never kiss a boy I'd not be marrying."

"It doesn't matter," he said. Without argument he waived his claim.

"It isn't that I'm not fond of you," she repeated, fearing he was hurt. "It's a promise I made, a vow. I couldn't break it."

Michael stroked her hand. "It's all right. I'm not worrying because I mustn't kiss you. I'll do anything you say. It's this other trouble. I want to marry you. Oh, God, I want to marry you, Cathleen!"

"And I want you to, Michael. Won't you try to be a Catholic? If I give you a prayer, will you say it? God will change your unbelief, and everything will be all right."

"You don't understand, my dear. I can't pray. It would be hypocrisy. I don't believe there's anyone to pray to."

"What a wicked boy you are!" cried Cathleen, fondly scolding.

"But, Cathleen, listen. You don't understand how I feel about these things. I must be faithful to my convictions, mustn't I?"

"Not if they're wrong," she said firmly. The shadow of despair darkened his face. "Never

31

mind, dear Michael. Let's be happy while we can."

"Let's go and get some tea." He rose, and helped her up.

There was a moment of sweet anguish for Michael when, in the teashop, the landlady had left them to themselves, and he watched Cathleen pour out the tea. He had never before sat with her in such domestic intimacy; nor seen her with her hat off. He imagined themselves married and in their own home, and the longing to kiss her lips almost overwhelmed him. Almost, but not quite. Cathleen allowed him to enfold her, to touch her cheek with his own. With his smooth face he stroked the down, the marvellous bloom, of her white neck. Tantalizing himself, he put his lips to hers in the shadow of a kiss. And yet he did not kiss her.

IV

Subsequent days brought more hours of poignant joy. Michael's leave dwindled to vanishing point. When he and Cathleen were together, not even the thought of approaching doom, the death-in-life of separation, could quench their delight in each other. Like waifs tossed together in mid-ocean, they clung in bliss until the unappeasable tides of the world should come to cleave them for ever asunder. So Michael saw their situation; but Cathleen was buoyed up by a secret belief which he, more clear-sighted, could not entertain. She believed that sooner or later her Michael would find his way into the arms of the one true Church, and so into her own arms never to be loosed.

The last day of the world dawned in splendour. She was shut up in her post office, he knew, until seven o'clock ; but at five, unable to endure another moment's inactivity, he stepped out of his cottage and turned his face towards her.

Ten yards away, he met her. His heart shouted with joy. She had got time off for him. They had two hours added to their precious evening. . . . But a second glance at her face checked his ecstasies.

" Oh, Michael ! "

" Darling, what is it ? "

" I've got to do telegraphs to-night."

Before she could continue he cried out : " Telegraphs ! Is our last night to be laid waste by telegraphs ! " Despair, like a cold toad, sat upon his heart.

" Sally has been called away." Sally was the dumpy friend. " Her mother's very ill."

" The goblin ! Do goblins have mothers ? "

" Don't be cruel, Michael. I must be back at closing time."

" Come back to the cottage," he said, pre-occupied with disappointment. " Unless you'd rather walk ? "

She looked at him gravely, trying to veil the surprise in her eyes ; and she knew at once that he did not realize the magnitude of what he had

2

asked of her. Such innocence could only be matched by generosity, no matter what it cost her.

"No," she answered firmly. "I'd rather sit down." But she could not repress a pang of fear as she entered the cottage door. Had she been seen? Was her reputation already being butchered by the village gossips?

Once inside, alone with her joy and her pain, she cast fear aside. Time slipped away, and it seemed to Michael that all the best of life, all beauty, all delight, was slipping with it. Cathleen sat on a hassock at his feet and rested her head in his lap. With the bitterness of parting already in his mouth, he felt upon his shoulders all the illimitable tragedy of life—exquisite burden. Here was his one chance of love, and it was passing. To-morrow he would be too old for love.

He bent over her yearningly, raised her a little in his arms; and his hands fondled her firm full breasts. He felt himself drowning in the bliss of her body's loveliness.

"Oh, Cathleen, do love me!"

She looked up, tender, distressed, struggling with herself. "I'm crazy about you, Mick. Kiss me!" For an immortal moment she yielded her lips to him with passion.

He became divinely mad. "Love me! Do love me!"

She had given all she dared. "I must really go now. Let me go, darling!"

She rose; tidied her hair; put on her hat. They kissed again, in farewell.

"You'll write to me, Michael?"

"Yes, I'll write," he said, still trembling.

They tried to smile at each other.

"Oh, Michael, I must tell you. I thought to hide it, but I can't. I'm being transferred to Ireland next month. The order came through yesterday."

To Michael, pent in the City of London, Ireland would be infinitely remote. He could not speak.

"But we must meet again, mustn't we? You'll say that prayer I gave you, Michael? Then everything will come right for us."

He wanted to cry out "Go! Go!" But he still smiled with grey lips. "I'll try, Cath."

"Good-bye."

"Good-bye."

She was gone, out of sight at last. Michael stepped back to his cottage door, staggered against the lintel, and hid his face from the light. He felt utterly beaten and forlorn, like an abandoned child. Yet when, the first fury of grief spent, he went into his bedroom, it was not the face of a child that he saw in the mirror, but that of a haggard youth, with age in his eyes and dark semicircles under them.

He went to the window and leaned out towards the horizon. Hours passed without sound. The sky hung over him like a luminous curtain of green shading into a less luminous blue, in which one tiny puncture, the first star, flashed and faded and flashed again like a dagger's point. The infinite spaces were emptied of meaning for him ; mute and still, they were but the symbol of an everlasting indifference. The evening light seemed unearthly, tinting all things with a colour that made the green grass darkly vivid and the hedges a dim purple. In the field just below him, beyond the patch of kitchen-garden, old George Proudfoot bent over his mowing, pausing from time to time to spit on his hands and stare at the world's rim. For a moment Michael's glance rested on that ancient man, dignified only in labour ; and in the boy's un-listening ears sounded the sibilant unfaltering rhythm of moving sickle and falling grass.

v

In the Manager's Room of the City and Counties Bank, Oxford Street, old Mr Turner, with a polite official expression fixed on his well-preserved, clean-shaven face, spent ten seconds or less in his endeavour to recall the peculiar significance of his client's Christian name. Other thoughts soon wandered aimlessly across his mind. His wife that morning had had the beginnings of a cold in the head. He hoped it had not developed. Annie was tiresome when anything ailed her : apt to sigh with unnecessary emphasis, and to make allusions, none too veiled, to his ill-success in business. She had wanted the eldest boy sent to Oxford ; she had wanted all manner of unattainable things. And she sniffed. It was always a discomfort having people with colds about the house. A pity she sniffed. A pity she bullied her servant. Yet she was necessary : the thought of life without her was not to be entertained. They had ways and tastes and a handful of ideas in common. Each to the other was an ineradicable habit, and he recognized the fact not only without bitterness, but with a certain positive satisfaction.

Corbett interrupted his musing by bringing in the safe-custody receipt made out for his signature. Corbett, smart junior, had been out of the room a bare three minutes, during which time neither Mr Turner nor his venerable client had said a word. Mr Turner, once more the complete bank official, affixed his signature with an accustomed gesture.

" And that is your receipt, Mrs Severn."

" Thank you," she said, receiving it from his hand. Laboriously she read it through. She rose to her feet unsteadily, helped by her stick. " I do hope my taxi hasn't run off without me."

Mr Turner opened the door for her. " Allow me," he said, presenting his arm.

They passed out together into the public office. When they reached the swing-doors that gave upon the street he stood aside to let her pass out ; then followed to escort her to the waiting taxi.

Seated in the taxi, she bent forward to thank him. He bowed courteously over her mittened hand, and looking up, met the glance in her blue eyes. " So kind of you," she said. " I'm not so young as I was, Michael."

37

The taxi had moved away before it occurred to him to wonder. For a few moments he stood, lost in dreams; then he went back to his duties. "Well, well, well," said Mr Turner. "Now *there's* a strange thing."

From "The Baker's Cart"

THE BAKER'S CART

FATHER was again in disgrace. Mother was once more beet-red with indignation. "My dear!" cried he in bewilderment . . . but even that was turned against him. If only he'd *dear* less and *do* more! Mother was as skilful in debate as in housekeeping: waste was abhorrent to her, whether of words or of half-pennies. Her habit in controversy was to stab out with one phrase, and then remain silent for a period of days. Father, divining that such a period was about to begin, lost no time in venting his anger, not upon the cause of it, but upon nine-year-old Harriet bending in terror over her porridge, upon the green venetian blinds, the wallpaper, the *Pears' Annual* pictures, and all the appurtenances of the breakfast room in which they sat, husband, wife, and youngest daughter. He declared that the wallpaper was poisonous, that the pictures were hung crooked, and that the architect who planned french windows to open on a backyard littered with drains was an imbecile.

"Take your hair out of your plate, Harriet," he said, in parenthesis.

The ghost of a smile played and passed over the face of Mother, a smile which Harriet inter-

39

preted as full and free forgiveness of Father's reference to the wallpaper of her choice, and to the pictures her hands had hung. For Mother was always thinking of others, self-abnegation being the most conspicuous of her virtues. Harriet expected her every moment to say to the culprit, as she had so often said to her children : "It is not of me you must ask pardon, but of Him above."

At the moment Father seemed disinclined to ask pardon of anyone. He continued his indictment of Number 27, Coniston Villas, and extended its application until the whole universe appeared clouded with his displeasure. He inquired, with some bitterness, why Alice and Maud were not at breakfast. Incredible blunder ; for Alice and Maud, those hardworked elder sisters of Harriet, had broken their fast and hurried away to their dingy City offices fully fifteen minutes before he, their erring father, had emerged from his so-called workroom. It was not often *they* had a Saturday off, oh no ! Mother could not forbear to break her strategic silence with this information.

The storm of Father's angry eloquence rose and fell and rose again, until, presently, he seemed to gulp it back. He pushed away his plate with such violence that the bacon fat he had left upon it became a turbulent sea, whose waves washed forward to the table-cloth and backward to the pushing fingers. Whereat he muttered an unknown word, wiped the offended finger on his napkin, and loped out of the room like an awkward schoolboy.

Mother heaved a deep sigh. She rose from the table with infinite dignity and, from the greater height, shot one keen, wistful glance at her daughter's bowed head. Harriet, though she kept her eyes averted, was conscious of that glance, which she knew to be a sign that Mother's cross was almost more than she could bear, and that Mother's little girl must comfort Mother by being very good and sweet and helpful, particularly in respect of the dirty breakfast things. But Harriet chose to ignore the appeal. She allowed Mother unaided to pile up the plates and gather together the knives and forks ; and when, a few minutes later, Mother returned from the kitchen with a tray, Harriet was lying on her back under the table. The defection cost her a pang. She knew that, given the opportunity, Mother would pet and praise her, and say what a blessing she was. It was very nice to be a blessing ; and Mother was so dear and adorable, with her lovely olive skin and her eyes of tenderness, that she could not be resisted. Harriet, on the few occasions that she had tried to resist, had always finally surrendered with tears and contrite kisses : it was as though Mother, by the very abundance of her love, levied tribute on this miraculous child of her middle-age. What could Harriet do but love the mother to whom she owed so much, the mother who fed and clothed her, played with her, told her stories, and slaved,

2*

for her sake and her sisters', to keep the home together? "We'll have no secrets from each other, will we, Babs dear! I want to know everything, *everything*, that goes on in that funny little brown head of yours." Mother loved her voraciously, and wished not to share her, even with Alice and Maud, still less with Father, whose mysterious wickedness it was—violent temper, lack of ambition, love of idle hobbies and unproductive dreaming—that threatened the home with disruption. Harriet feared her father almost as much as she loved her mother. She hated him sometimes, on her mother's behalf, for his unkindness. Yet even in the love she owed, and diligently paid, to her mother, there was a lurking and unrecognized fear. Something deep within her shrank from the ultimate surrender, something struggled against being absorbed into that other and so powerful personality. In spite of the maternal edict, Harriet did withhold secrets: trivial, childish things, thoughts and hopes of less than gossamer substance; yet they were precious to her, the more so because they were intimately, inviolably, her very own. "You're such a nice baby, I could gobble you up," cried Mother in her raptures; "all your youth and freshness. They make *me* a child again, you little mousie!" And though it was great fun to be gobbled up with kisses, Harriet contrived to withhold her innermost treasure from the insatiable heart that laid siege to it.

Under the table she lay at peace, fancying herself a princess, the four table-legs the posts of a great, royal bed, and the underside of the table the dim purple canopy. Then she began playing the most secret and delicious of all her games, which she called Going Inside. Inside was her peculiar paradise. It was tingling, glowing, a riot of lonely colours in perpetual motion. It was a little wood where squirrels sat nibbling nuts on the green banks of a stream that trickled, with jewel clarity, over a pebbly bed ; a region where, beyond time and space, the eternal fairy-tales mingled in spontaneous fantasy. It was fragrant to the nostrils, comforting to the palate, a refuge for the mind. It smelt of honeysuckle and pines and moist earth ; it tasted like a precious stone. And Mother had never been there.

From this country of the mind, after a few moments, Harriet was dragged back, abruptly, to a consideration of her father and his misdeeds ; and as she pondered the mystery an adventurous impulse moved in her. Father was now, she guessed, in that little shed at the bottom of the garden which he called, to Mother's disgust, his workroom ; the place where, in idle moments, he carved and chipped and carpentered to his heart's content. She did not love Father, because he did not deserve to be loved ; but to-day the mystery of his personality excited her a little. She resolved, with a sudden intake of the breath, to visit the baffling creature in its own iniquitous den.

II

Father was at work with a long, flexible saw. He was red in the face, and emitting little grunts of exertion. Sometimes the saw, having reached the end of its outgoing journey, refused to be pulled back, and then the tapering end seemed like a ripple of steel-grey water. Father paused, mopped his brow, and flung a surprised glance at Harriet, who stood shyly in the doorway.

" Well, and what are you after ? " His tone was uninviting.

Harriet hung her head. " I don't know."

" Did your mother send you with a message ? "

" No," said Harriet. " I just wanted to see. . . . Oh, Father, what a lovely work-house you've got ! "

Father permitted himself to grin. " You've seen it often enough before, haven't you ? "

" I haven't *really*, you know," explained Harriet. " I've just sort of looked a tiny peep ; that's all."

" You're sure your mother didn't send you ? " said Father, suspicion reappearing in his eye.

" Trufa-nonna ! " declared Harriet, earnestly. " I just thought I'd look you up, don't you see."

Father laughed. " You're a rum child. Want to see what's going on, eh ? "

Harriet nodded. " What are you making, Father ? "

" Making nothing at present. Sawing up

44

planks for use later on. But I made something this morning. Like to see it?"

" Yes, please," answered Harriet, dissembling her delight.

" But it's a secret, mind!"

It didn't seem to matter, after all, that she did not love Father. This warm comfortable feeling inside her was so much better than love. Here was Father, that bad man, about to tell her a secret. That was a thing that Mother had never done. Mother extracted confidences, but never gave them. This was different, this new experience, and much more exciting. Father, knowing nothing of commerce, was unbosoming himself without demanding anything. Harriet was enchanted by his curtness, his casualness, his man-to-man air.

" It's a little thing I've invented," said Father, with engaging vanity. " A mangle, you see. You clamp it down to the kitchen table with these two screws; and this roller travels over the board and back again, squeezing the clothes dry. See? All you have to do is to turn this handle."

" Oo!" cried Harriet. And she added, with her most ladylike and adult air: " Did you make it all this morning, every teeny bit of it?"

" Well, no," admitted the inventor. " Not exactly all. I had the roller done yesterday, and the board partly done. But I ribbed the board this morning, and fitted the whole thing together. Got up three hours earlier so's to get it done before breakfast. It was to be a surprise, don't you see."

Magic phrase! "A surprise. Who for? For Mother?"

Father shrugged his shoulders. "It's here when she wants it."

Harriet understood; but she remained silent, nodding wisely.

"I suppose," she ventured, "you couldn't make something for me, could you? You haven't time, I expect."

Father's queer smile gave her courage to be more explicit.

"I do so want something. It isn't a very big thing."

"Well, what is it?" demanded Father gruffly, becoming very busy with the saw once more.

"Only a baker's cart," pleaded Harriet. "Is it very hard to make a baker's cart?"

"Baker's cart!" said Father, with unashamed conceit. "Easiest thing in the world, a baker's cart is. You watch, my dear!"

He strode over to his scrap-heap, hovered for a moment in contemplation, and then pounced on some pieces of wood. "Now, here we are. Let's get to work with the fret-saw." He got to work with the fret-saw, and with a hammer and tiny tintacks. "There you are—there's the beginning of your cart! Nice high cart bakers live in, with big yellow wheels, or do you prefer green wheels?"

"Red wheels," said Harriet.

"Red as blood," agreed Father, in his excitement. "And now we'll make a partition here, and a dropboard fastened up with hooks and eyes like all the best dropboards. . . . Now that little place is where the loaves go, see."

"Oo, the loaves!"

"Quite so. *Oo the loaves* is what the baker calls out; at least, ours does. He calls out just as he jumps off the step of his cart. Now, where shall we find something for a step? Two steps, in fact. One each side."

"And wheels? What are we going to make the wheels of?"

But Father had already cut out two circular discs of thin wood.

"But they must have spokes!" objected Harriet.

"A very fair criticism," admitted Father. "Spokes they shall have. We arrive at spokes by a process of elimination. Thus!" He sketched out the spokes with his stump of fat pencil—that fascinating pencil!—and again set to work with the fret-saw.

Harriet began to dance up and down, clapping her hands, as the baker's cart took shape before her eyes. Her slim, black-stockinged legs twinkled as she darted to and fro amid the litter of carpentry. These outbursts were rare: lyrical and irrepressible. For the most part she stood in speechless rapture, large eyes shining with joy from her peaked, elfish face.

"After lunch, a coat of paint," said Father, gazing at his creation with pardonable satisfaction.

III

Mother stood in the doorway of the shed. She was displeased.

"Harriet! I've been looking for you everywhere. What are you doing here, hindering your father in his work?"

"Only just watching, Mother."

"Well, run along now and get your things on. I'm going to visit the Cottage Hospital. There's just time before lunch. You'd like to come with me, wouldn't you, darling?"

"Yes," said Harriet, without enthusiasm.

On the way into the house Mother asked: "What is that new toy you've got there, dear? Show Mother."

Harriet's fist reluctantly yielded up its treasure. "A baker's cart."

"A baker's cart. Aren't you getting a little too old for bakers' carts, Harriet? Where did you get it?"

"Father made it for me."

"Indeed!" Mother's tone was chillier than ever. "Be quick and get your boots buttoned up, my child."

On the way to the Cottage Hospital, to which every few weeks it was Mother's habit to take a basket of bounty, she talked to Harriet about the duty of kindness to those less fortunately circumstanced than ourselves. "We're going to see those poor little orphans, Harriet. You remember?"

Harriet remembered.

"Just a few dainties I'm taking them," said Mother, blithely. "It will give them so much pleasure, poor dears!"

Harriet agreed, her eyes moistening.

"Now isn't there any little thing you'd like to give?" said Mother, persuasively. "There's poor Tommy Fish, who had that dreadful operation and will never be able to walk again. Think what that means, Harriet."

Harriet, clutching her mother's hand, trotted along in dumb distress.

"It would be nice to brighten the little fellow's life, wouldn't it, dear, if only for a day or two?"

"Oh, Mother," said Harriet. "Shall I go back and fetch my Noah's Ark. I'm too old for that now, aren't I?"

"Yes, dear. But it's not very kind to give away only the things we don't want ourselves, is it?"

Harriet grew red with shame. "What shall I give him, Mother?"

"I don't want to influence you," said Mother. "It is for you to decide. A real sacrifice. If you feel you can. Now, if I were you . . . there's this pretty little baker's cart."

"But that's at home," said Harriet, quickly.

Mother produced the baker's cart from her muff. "No, dear. Here it is."

" Oh, dear, he can't have that ! He shan't ! "

" A poor little orphan, Harriet."

Harriet whimpered. " I want it myself. I do. I've wanted it a long time. I don't believe Him above will mind me keeping it. I've got so many other things that I wouldn't miss. And Tommy Fish'd like them just as well."

" It's not only Tommy I'm thinking of, darling. It's you too. It is more blessed to give, you know. . . . But, of course, I shan't force you."

Resentment, anger, fear, and despair : these in turn were Harriet's dominant emotions as they finished their walk to the Cottage Hospital. Admitted to the convalescent ward, Mother distributed her gifts, going from bed to bed like an angel of mercy. Finally she paused at the foot of a bed where a pale-faced urchin lay stretched on his back grinning gallantly whenever a visitor addressed him.

" Here's Tommy Fish," said Mother. " How are you this morning, Tommy ? "

Tommy's boast of being much better this morning was cut short by a twinge of pain.

Harriet's lip quivered. She turned away her face and nudged her mother. " Give it to him, please, Mother."

" Are you quite sure——" began Mother.

" Yes. I want him to have it." A moment ago Harriet had hated Tommy Fish. But now she burned with hatred for something else, she knew not what, some shadowy thing that had made irony of the boy's cheerful answer.

"Tommy, my Harriet has brought you something. Just a little toy."

Harriet hid her flaming face during this ceremony. She wanted nothing but release from this house of torment. She tugged at her mother's arm.

To step into the open air again was like waking from an evil dream. Mother was still talkative, though subdued. As they entered the house she asked : " Are you glad, dear, or sorry that you parted with your little cart ? "

" Glad," whispered Harriet.

" That's right." Harriet's mother was moved, perhaps by compunction. Her voice trembled a little.

" Tommy Fish is an orphan, isn't he, Mother ? That means he hasn't got a father, doesn't it ? "

" Yes, dear. No mother or father."

" Oh," cried Harriet, " I'm so glad he had my baker's cart. 'Cause I've still got Father, haven't I ? "

Mother's face flamed, and paled as swiftly. She clenched her hands, and her eyes faltered as they strove to meet the innocent gaze of Harriet. She knew herself defeated.

From "The Baker's Cart"

THE GRASSHOPPER

To walk from one side of the room to another
was now as hazardous an undertaking for
Paul Stevenage as it had been ninety years
before when first he had stood erect upon this
whirling globe; and he regretted the queer
impulse that had prompted him to bolt his
cottage door last night, when, on the eve of his
birthday, he had been visited by an intimation,
the first of its kind, that the weakness as well
as the pride of age was descended upon him.
Bodily weakness he had been long familiar with;
but this misgiving, this pang of loneliness, presented a strange face. Chewing a long cud of
memories, living in a past more real to him than
the sunshine that was urgent at his window,
more real than the beardless generation passing
his door, what should he know of loneliness?
Yet now a kind of fear whispered in his mind.
That's gone, that's past, ran the message, and
I'm left here alone. He was more than ever
alone, now that the common delights were
failing him. For years past he had sat in his
doorway, every fine day, and watched the
comings and goings in the little lane; but increasingly, of late, he had found the air too cool,
even in summer, or the sun too strident in its

brightness. Sunlight quivering on the chalky road was like a loud noise; the patter of rain-drops on the window-pane made him wince; and the village children seemed rowdier every day. The outer world, indeed, was at once more clamorous and less significant, less intel-ligible, than it had been in former times. It was always knocking at his door, and to no good purpose. It was knocking now, with an iteration that seemed hostile and induced in him, as he made the slow difficult journey across the room, an answering hostility.

A voice outside announced, somewhat im-patiently: " Postman ! "

Breathless from bending to unfasten the bolt, he had no greeting for the postman, but received without a word the packet thrust into his hands. He let the door remain open, and returned to his chair to think things over. It was his birthday. Yesterday, until the moment of that tremor in the soul, he had conceived it as a day of triumph; had in fancy received over and over again the congratulations of his neighbours. He knew himself to be a prodigy, being, in spite of his feebleness, still able to see and hear as well as any youngster of sixty. He knew himself for a wonderful old man; but, greatly as he had enjoyed the part in the past, he was now a little tired of it. The day was begun; in a short while the curtain would go up on what had promised to be the finest scene in the play; but there would be no performance. Paul, his courage at the ebb, felt in his bones that he would never be a wonderful old man again.

There were so many difficult things to do. There was, for example, when he remembered it, this packet to open. It was tied with string and sealed with red wax. The prospect of opening his jack-knife, cutting the string, unfolding the brown paper, and examining the contents of the packet—this in anticipation so cruelly fretted him that he wished he had stayed in bed and slept through the postman's knocking. From time to time he would forget the thing altogether and lose himself agreeably in reverie, but always, in the end, he came back to it, lying there in his lap, demanding attention. Finally, by a prodigious effort of the will, he set to work. The knife was in his trousers pocket, to reach which he had to uncross his legs and straighten his body from the hip downwards—a tedious business. Then the knife must be opened and the string cut. He went over the process three times in fancy before he achieved it in fact: three several times, divided by intervals of dreaming and of wishing it were over and done with. At last, with the sense of having got through a day's work and more than a day's worry, he came to the heart of the matter. From the piece of cardboard that his tired fingers held, a pretty girl of about seventeen looked pertly up at him. He returned her gaze, at first dully, without interest, and then, as recognition half-dawned, with a faint wonder stirring at his heart.

Some chord in him was touched, but not awakened, and he vaguely felt, rather than thought, that somewhere in the remote past this face had been known to him. There was a letter accompanying the photograph :

> Just a lines to wish you hapy reterns and a liknis of our grandorter daisy who you of never seen our dear son George quit a scholard as writen this letter i shall soon be 81 of age dear Paul from dear Dot.

He was greatly puzzled by this letter, which gave hints of a story to which he had somehow lost the key. Dot he remembered, because he had seen her as recently as fifteen years ago, in her native village ten miles distant from his own, and it was of her, he supposed, that the young woman in the photograph reminded him. But the phrase " our dear son George " was meaningless to the old man ; and, fatigued by the brief effort to understand it, he allowed the letter to fall unheeded to the floor, and his mind drifted on to other thoughts.

He was roused by the entry of young Mrs Haycock, the brisk and comfortable woman of fifty who occupied the adjoining cottage and came in each day to get his meals for him. This morning she was radiant with consciousness of the great occasion.

" Well, there you are ! " she cried, rubbing her hands on her apron. " Ninety-two to-day. Many 'appy returns, I'm sure, Granfer ! "

Paul mumbled an acknowledgment; then, pointing at the letter, which he happened at that moment to catch sight of on the floor, he said accusingly: "Our dear son George, she says. What can she mean be that, eh?"

Mrs Haycock, having picked up the letter and mastered its contents, began laying the breakfast table in silence, as though she had quite lost interest in the subject. But presently she remarked, in the tone one uses to a child: "George? Why that must be George Robins, your own son, if all accounts be true. You know your son George, him that come to see you a year or two back. You must know 'im. Old George Robins. Why, everybody knows George."

She did not appear to expect any reply, but presently, having slowly digested her information, he remarked: "My son, George Robins? Yes, I mind 'im." After a silence he added pettishly: "But what's George to do with Dot?"

Mrs Haycock approached with a steaming cup of tea. "She's 'is mother by the look of things, though it's none of my business. And this pretty gel's 'is daughter." She bent over the photograph, and, having gazed her fill, summed up her admiration of it in one long sigh.

"Ah," said Paul, sipping his tea reflectively, "Dot were young George's mother, so she were. I'd got 'im mixed up with another gel." He creased up his face in a strange show of mirth, and a chuckle that was all but silent shook his frail frame. "Eh, but that'll be sixty year ago, I'll lay."

Paying little or no heed to this remark, Mrs Haycock said, with loud, sick-room cheerfulness: "If you eat your breakfast nicely, Granfer, I've got a little surprise for you." She paused at the door to repeat: "A little surprise I'm fetching for you."

"I ain't deaf," answered Paul, bending over his plate. "What makes gels so bloody noisy?" he inquired, of the world at large. But when Mrs Haycock reappeared a moment later, carrying her "little surprise" with her, the old man remembered his manners in time to say: "Thank ye kindly, me dear. Very thoughtful and nice." He did not as yet know what form the gift was taking, but he was eager to get his thanks said without delay, lest subsequent events should put them out of his mind. He watched, with a curiosity that threatened to become irritation, while Mrs Haycock, mysteriously smiling, placed a large square parcel on the brick floor. "Now you'll see!" she promised him. With these words she spat a long nail into her hand, whipped a hammer from her apron pocket, and, with these preparations made, eyed appraisingly the oak beam that ran across the ceiling. "That's the place for it," said Mrs Haycock, after due deliberation. "But you'll have to mind not to knock your head on it, Granfer."

Her assault with hammer and nail upon his

home was more than Paul could bear without protest; but he was appeased when her intention became clear; and when at last the bird in its cage was safely suspended from the ceiling, he was moved to say, in all sincerity: "That's a martal pretty bird, me dear." It was, indeed, the prettiest creature that Paul had ever seen: sleek, plump, bright-eyed, in form the embodiment of grace, in colour the most delicate satin green. "And do he sing?" asked Paul.

Mrs Haycock was eloquent in its praise, but it was the bird itself, after she had gone, that—in a burst of golden song—answered Paul's question. He was startled with joy by the suddenness with which the room filled with passion and beauty. Sunlight and green fields and running water were in that bird's voice, so that Paul, listening, felt spring-time quicken in his veins and the heart lifted out of him in ardour and aspiration. When silence fell he cried: "Sweet, sweet!" trying by conventional bird language to coax from the lovely creature another song. And so it sang again and again, recreating in a shimmer of intricate melody the paradise from which it was exiled, and of which the sunshine, entering the open doorway, brought thrilling intimations. The old man listened, first in delight, then sadly. Sadness gave place to the realization that he was weary of this incessant noise; it was too loud, it was shouting words inside his head, and if he could not get relief from it he must cry with vexation. "It's nesting time, don't you see," Mrs Haycock had complacently said. "So of course the lil thing be full of song." He recalled this saying, muttering it to himself without being aware of its meaning, while he laboriously rose from his chair and faltered across the room to where the caged bird hung. He approached the bird with intention, but forgot the intention before it could be fulfilled, its place in his mind being smoothly, stealthily appropriated by moments of the past: of himself as a child catching and killing the flies on a cow's back; chance glimpses of meadow and sky; boys in a brook, splashing and fighting; a strange summer night spent in Venner's Wood with a girl whose face he had long forgotten; and of ploughing, ploughing, with the broad equine buttocks swaying in front of him, and the tail twitching, and the furrows multiplying, and heat beating tangibly from the sky and rising visibly in a quivering glaze from the ground, and the soft thud of hoofs, the gliding furrow, the smell of the newly sliced earth all mingling in his senses. These things came to him neither vivid nor dim; they were clear and bright, but they lacked the sharpness that made so troublesome the actual and present world, their light being veiled as by silk, their sounds muffled, their outlines softened by distance and uncertainty. The little rivers of this country soundlessly enamelled their pebbly beds; its sun did not scorch, nor its cold winds bite. Kisses kindled no fire, and the

mingling of limbs meant neither pleasure nor
regret. Everything was subdued to the quality
of quiet daydreaming, particular memories being
rare and few in a stream made up for the most
part of images without form and echoes without
sound. The outer world intruded but little into
this reverie, so quick was the mind to translate
the intruder into terms of the subtler medium ;
the breath of honeysuckle that entered the room
set stirring in Paul's heart a symphony of spring-
time to which numerous vanished and unremem-
bered seasons contributed ; and this very bird,
even while he gazed at it, was lost for a while in
the anonymous multitude of sensations that its
singing evoked.

But now the green bird, with shrill cries,
began beating itself against the wires of its cage,
and Paul's dreams scattered suddenly under this
assault of reality. The noise and violence hurt
him ; every nerve in his frail body was unendur-
ably jarred ; his head filled with screaming and
mirthless laughter. Into this pandemonium
there flashed the thought, beautiful as the
promise of salvation, that, if he could not silence
the creature in any other way, he could at least
twist its damned neck ; and at once his fingers
quivered to be at their murderous work. Dizzy
with the effort to stand up straight, dangerously
swaying on his feet like a little child, he yet
maintained his precarious balance long enough
to be able to touch the cage with fumbling hands.
But the cage door so cunningly resisted his

attempts to open it that a feeble fury shook him —tears of vexation rose in his throat, shooting pains darted in and out of his eyes, and it was as if a band of hot steel had been clamped about his throbbing temples. Had he had but the power he would have torn the cage from the ceiling and trampled it madly under foot. In imagination he saw himself doing so, and this picture of his former strength distracted him a little from his present anger; for, whatever he was now become, he had been a tidy enough chap in his day, as the village girls in terror and delight freely admitted when a mad dog came snapping and snarling down the street to be neatly strangled by fingers that were now too weak to open a bird-cage.

Having lost himself again in memories, he woke with surprise to the knowledge that the cage-door was open and the bird gone. But the sound of its singing still vibrated in the sunlit room, and he looked round in time to see a green light circle once round the room, with agitated wings, before finding its way to freedom through the open door. After seeing the bird vanish, the old man stood motionless for a moment, as though bathing his spirit in the pool of super-vening silence, his eyes staring at the sunlit picture of spring which the doorway framed for him. Then, with a sigh, he struggled back to his chair and sank down, wondering where the green bird would have led him if he had followed it. Perhaps into a singing forest and over the green

hills that lay beyond; perhaps, indeed, to
Venner's Wood itself, or along the grass-grown
Roman road that ran round the bases of the three
hills, down Cuffield way. The better to picture
such adventuring, Paul closed his eyes; and
the sun streamed down upon him, and the
white road was solid under his feet. His sight
was keen and clear, his step was elastic, and he
smiled with satisfaction to feel the vigour that
pulsed in his veins. The light streaming up
from the road delighted his eyes without dazzling
them; he felt confident, equal to anything; and,
as he ran his fingers through the noble white
beard that now stretched as far as the lowest
button of his waistcoat, he chuckled and cried
aloud: "I be a wonderful old man, there's no
denying!" He became aware, then, of a
powerful thirst raging within him, and at the
same moment, by a happy chance he reached
the summit of the hill and found himself staring
at an old tavern sign, which he spelled out to
himself letter by letter: *The King of Heaven*. It
was a heartening sight, this tavern, beautiful and
ancient in design, mellow in colouring, fragrant
with the suggestion of harvest and sunset and
that quiet good fellowship which the heart
desires after a long and lonely journey; a
heartening sight, and to a thirsty man like Paul
more than heartening. In a trice he had lifted
the latch of the door and stepped in. The
interior of the tavern warmed his heart with
sudden pleasure; he felt intensely at home;

yet he was aware that to all the old familiar things that his eyes now gratefully encountered, in their slow wondering scrutiny of the place, there was added a something at once very beautiful and a little strange that he had not expected to find there. A curious light, as of an eternal morning, filled this tavern; and it was perhaps the quality of this light that made him forget for a moment that he must quench that fine thirst of his. At his entry a comely and kindly young woman rose to greet him with a smile of old friendship. An aureole of light encircled her dark head, and her eyes were bluer than a fair sky in June, so that Paul, meeting their glance, lost himself for a while in those heavenly distances. But at last, scratching his head in bewilderment, he asked respectfully:

"Can I get a drop o' mild here, ma'am?"

"Surely," said the girl, with a laugh. She reached down a tankard, saying: "A quart?" It was wonderful the way she understood him. He began going through his pockets in search of coins, but she, observing the movement, remarked quietly: "There's nothing to pay here, you know. Like a bit of cheese with it?"

With his tankard in one hand and his plate of bread and cheese in the other, Paul made his way to the black, high-backed settle, and sat down. Over the pewter brim, as he emerged from his first draught, so deep and cool and satisfying, he saw the face of Dan Thatcher smiling at him. The two men nodded to each other, and, without need of words, everything was as it had been threescore years before.

"Warm to-day," mumbled Paul, through a mouthful of cheese.

"Ay," said Dan. "But a smart lil bit of wind on the 'ill 'ere."

There followed a long and comfortable silence, at the end of which Dan Thatcher rose, saying : "Well, cricket saternoon, 'spose ?" Without waiting for an answer he stamped his way out of the room.

Paul, remembering his age, grinned ruefully, and stroked his beard in protest. For the first time in this blessed place the wings of melancholy brushed him, but at that moment his attention was attracted by the sound of a lifted latch, and, turning in his seat, he saw the inner door of the taproom open, and heard the girl's voice saying : "Paul's come to see us at last."

There came into view, round the door's edge, the head and shoulders of an ancient, white-bearded man, whose radiant face lit up with a new pleasure at sight of Paul. As the stranger came into the room, carrying a newspaper in his hand, Paul knew him at once for what he was, and stood up humbly, with bowed head. After a moment of anguish and exultation he felt his two arms seized in a friendly grip ; and, looking upon the face of God the Father, he saw such age as made himself the veriest child, such youth as he had never known, a power that terrified him, and a charity that made him weep.

"Well, old friend," said God the Father. "Sit down again and let's take a drink together."

Paul, obeying, could only stammer out: "Where am I, Lord? Am I in heaven?"

"Where else?" said God the Father. He smiled at Paul; he smiled at the girl; and Paul became suddenly aware of a picture that hung on the wall at her back, a picture glowing with green fields and sparkling water, in which moved all the beloved figures of his past. Springing up to examine it more closely he saw that it was indeed no picture. It was a window that looked out upon the veritable kingdom of happiness. But while he stood, with held breath, and gazed, peace like an everlasting anthem flooding his heart, he heard a discordant screaming, and the walls of his cottage grew up darkly about him. Mrs Haycock was stroking his temples, saying cheerfully: "That's better now! Why, you give me quite a turn!" Looking past her, Paul could see the green bird standing pertly in the doorway; and, filled with old alarm, he cried out in a cracked, quavering voice: "Don't let the lil bird come back, missus. He do sing so loud, I can't bear un."

From "The World in Bud"

3   65

SUMMERS END

As for getting up early, Harriet would promise anything in the world if thereby she might have the adventure of riding with her uncle in a bumping wagon over the dim white roads and through the tingling air of morning.

"Ever so early I'll be ready," said Harriet, at the tea-table, "if only you'll wake me up, uncle. As early as early as early can be!"

Uncle Bob barked brief laughter, shaking his beard in the process, and screwing up his greenish eyes until they resembled the little rayed suns of the picture-book. Uncle Bob's eyes were at once fierce and kindly. He was broad and big and squat. His whiskers were so prodigious that they scarcely left room for the more personal features: like an abundant forest growing in red soil they flourished on chin and cheek and neck. Even from the broad nostrils they sprouted, though certainly with less decision. He was quite the hairiest man Harriet, at seven, had ever seen, and very nearly the nicest. He had a good crop of stories—rather terrible, earthy stories—though being merely human he could not compete with Harriet's father in this respect. He was rather like a huge friendly dog or a well-disposed bear: always ready in his leisure to romp and roar (indeed, his very speech was a roar), always smelling pleasantly of pigs or cowsheds. He was, in fact, the living symbol or epitome of Summers End in its homelier aspects : in him the farm—or at least the farmyard—had become flesh. He wore breeches and gaiters and fascinating leather cuffs attached to his sleeves. His clothes were the colour of the stale mustard that Harriet was accustomed to see in the cruet at home ; and his neck, exposed by an open shirt, was brick-red. He was the wildest man, as well as the hairiest, and he inspired Harriet not only with affection, but with a delicious fear. There was always the remote chance, too remote to be a source of positive terror, that he might one day grow extra hungry and eat her all up.

"What ! " shouted Uncle Bob, when his mirth had found adequate vent. "Be up at ha' past four, would you ? " From the tone and volume of his voice he might have been addressing the most recalcitrant of his cart-horses. "Ha' past four, *heigh* ? "

"Oo yes," cried Harriet. "As early as early as early can be," she chanted again.

Uncle Bob laughed once more. An easily amused man, Uncle Bob. "Earlyish for little gals, me dear ! Well, well, well ! "

He hastened to fill his mouth with an in-credible bite from a doorstep of bread-and-jam, pausing in mastication, a moment later, to pour a cupful of dark brown tea into that same accommodating cavity. He munched with energy, deftly reclaimed from his moustache some strayed particles both liquid and solid, and pushed back his chair. " Now then, Bert me boy ! "

Bert, grunting acquiescence, helped himself to a slab of cake, and took no notice of his father's stamping across the room. At the door the older man turned his head. " Milking," said father. " Ay," replied son. The mono-syllable struggled for utterance through a mouthful of cake.

Harriet liked Cousin Bert, if only because he, too, was part of Summers End and was invested with something of its glamour. She would perhaps have loved him had he been a shade less sulky. He seemed, she had to confess, sadly lacking in appreciation of the beautiful things and enchanting people by which he was sur-rounded. Harriet was not so absorbed in her sensations as to have no thought to spare for her friends, and she was quick to detect that Cousin Bert was not entirely at peace with his world. He had something on his mind. How else account for his long silences, his avoidance of Aunt Polly's searching glances, his failure to join in Uncle Bob's jollity, and his amazing indifference to all the happiness that pervaded Summers End like a smell ?—imperfect simile, for the smell itself was happiness, and happiness itself the fusion of sight and sound and smell. Not that Harriet worked the problem out, collecting evidence of Bert's disgruntlement and drawing a logical inference. No: she simply felt the discord in him and was timidly sorry about it. It was as definite and as unknown a quantity as would be a solid obstacle run into in the dark. Yet even Cousin Bert, infected by her new delight in the world, sometimes for brief spells emerged from the mysterious dream that commonly enveloped him. He had shown her the caged rabbits, being fattened for what purpose she knew not; had dug for her in the garden an elaborate system of canals, watered by the pump through rubber tubing; had instructed her in the art of spoon-feeding with worms the hens that clucked and scratched behind their wire-netting. Not perhaps a very pretty game, this last. It was conceivable that the worms did not enjoy it. But worms were such nasty things, and hens so lovely, that it was surely legitimate to please the one at the expense of the other, especially if one happened to please oneself at the same time. Cousin Bert, anyhow, made short work of her doubts. Yet she was conscious that his heart was neither in this nor in any of the other amusements he devised, from time to time, for her benefit. His interest in them manifestly lacked sincerity. A strange man, this Cousin Bert; a problem, indeed, though not an urgent one. Despite his great age—he approached twenty-two—Harriet felt maternally towards him. Bert, however, was already provided with a mother, known to his little cousin as Aunt

Polly ; and to mask his preoccupation from the watchful eyes of this mother was now his constant care. A sure instinct urged him to this secrecy : he knew that his mother was wise enough to understand his situation, but not young enough to enter into it imaginatively. He would not have expressed his conviction so, for it had become his habit to express himself mainly in grunts and growls and stubborn action ; but there the conviction was, at the bottom of his inarticulate soul. He was locked in the loneliness of adolescence.

"Now, darling," said Aunt Polly to Harriet, "finish up your tea."

Promptly Harriet removed her interested stare from her cousin's face, and began dabbing up the crumbs on her plate with a moistened forefinger. "No, Harriet : that's not the way. Eat nicely. Please do." Aunt Polly had a way with her that made one want to please her at whatever cost to one's own convenience. She made it a personal matter rather than one of discipline. She did not refer one to an ideal standard of behaviour : she appealed to one's compassion for her feelings. At once, with no interval of hesitation or disappointment, Harriet began eating "nicely," so anxious was she to oblige her beloved aunt. If Uncle Bob was the symbol of the farmyard, Aunt Polly was as certainly the cool, clean, delightful dairy made manifest. She was as plump as butter, as mild as milk ; she was placid and comfortable and

infinitely kind ; and she had scarcely more outward animation than one of her own cows.

" And after tea," said Aunt Polly, " shall we
do a little sewing together, you and I ? "

Harriet assented the more readily to this
proposal, which did not greatly attract her,
because she had, as she thought, already won
her point with Uncle Bob. She was to ride with
him, in those hours of the morning which she
had never before experienced, to fetch a load of
swedes for the cattle. She knew that there might
be earwigs in the wagon, but that was a possibility
one must face boldly. She need not, after all, sit
down : more fun, indeed, to stand and sway,
precariously balanced, with one eye on the
lolloping old mare and one on the diminishing
yet continuing ribbon of road, the pearly grey
sky, the smooth-gliding and fragrant hedges.
Already she seemed to feel the cart jolting under
her, to hear the metallic patter of the shod
hooves' contact with the ground, to see the broad
haunch and the swishing tail and the sharp equine
ears moving up and down in front of her. Already
little freshets of keen air, like fairy whips, stung
sharp colour into her cheeks. What mattered
earwigs ? Nasty though the creatures were,
their dangerousness was overrated. Once an
earwig had crept down her neck and secreted
himself under her camisole. A shocking
experience, fully justifying her passionate screams.
Yet she had survived it, and could survive it
again. She braced herself for the perilous ad-

venture, well content to be sojourning in a world
of which even the terrors did but add a flavour,
a queer zest, to the all-pervading jolliness.

II

Soon after Harriet had gone to bed Bert
Growcock returned from his final round of
farm duties to find his mother awaiting him.
She was knitting busily and gave no sign of
having noticed his entry, but he was not deceived. Sensitive to atmosphere in spite of
his dull looks, he was aware at once that she was
lying in wait for him ; and she, from whom he
had perhaps inherited his sensitiveness, was
instantly aware of his awareness. He knew that
she sought to invade his solitude ; she knew
that he would resist the invasion. No word was
said, but the air of the kitchen was quick with
the clash of their wills. He picked up the local
paper from the table, on which a light supper was
already set out, and sat down opposite her in a
creaking basket chair. The lamp shed a soft
yellow glow in the room. The hearth was
kindled, warm. On the varnished mantelpiece
a cheap marble clock, picked up at a recent sale,
monotonously ticked their lives away. The
mother bided her time. The son, uneasy,
shifted in his seat.

"Well," remarked Bert, running his eye
down his news sheet, " I suppose old Pappin's
dead at last."

" I suppose so," assented Mrs Growcock.

There was nothing at all suppositional about their belief in Pappin's death. They were employing a local turn of speech. The famous Pappin, full of years, was indubitably dead and buried, as the newspaper testified with much loquacity.

" Nice to see a bit of fire," observed Bert, after a longer silence.

" Yes. Summer's over before it's begun, this year. Never needed fires in September when I was a young woman. As Mrs Foster was saying only yesterday, the summer gets shorter every year."

Mrs Growcock quoted this remark only to comfort herself, knowing in her heart that it was untrue, and wishing by repetition to make it sound true. For what was happening had nothing to do with the seasons. Not in the stars, but in her blood, was the cause of this premature chilliness. She was no longer a young woman; every day her grasp on middle-age became more tenuous; and lately she had taken to thinking about herself and had found the process painful. She was aware of having worked very hard for a great number of years, worked and suffered and remained obstinately cheerful, paying dearly for every fugitive pleasure; and now, with a husband who took life too easily, and a son who took it too hard, she was constrained to wonder if anything had been worth while. If Bert, her only achievement, Bert, for whose life she had paid in blood and tears and toil and incessant prayerfulness—if he, too, missed happiness, she was cheated of all satisfaction, the dupe of nature and of hope.

" Rain about to-night," said Bert, " shouldn't wonder."

" . . . twenty-four, twenty-five," counted Mrs Growcock, casting off her stitches. " When are you thinking of getting married, Bert ? "

But she did not in the least take him by surprise. He had been momently expecting, if not just this, something equally uncompromising.

" No hurry for that," he returned easily. " Hardly old enough, am I ? "

" No, but you're young enough," said his mother shrewdly. " What does *she* think about it, my boy ? "

No match for her as a fencer, he was caught off his guard. " What, Lottie ? " he said eagerly. And frowned, realizing his blunder.

Mrs Growcock's black bone knitting-needles clattered on the tiled floor. When she had recovered them her face was flushed with the exertion of stooping. " Ay," she said, and her voice lacked its accustomed steadiness. " What does Lottie Marsh say about it ? "

" Maybe she's waiting till she's asked," suggested Bert. But his cunning was a minute too late. " Of course," he said, temper rising, " if you've been poking round, Mother, there's no more to be said." Shrugging his shoulders he made a great show of unfolding again the paper he had discarded.

" I haven't deserved that," she answered. Her face was unnaturally pale, her voice dispassionate. " A mother doesn't need to go poking round. Maybe I've no right to know your affairs, but when I see you making yourself miserable I use my eyes, that's all. Why not tell me about it and have done ? "

Seeing the emotion that she strove to conceal, and mistaking its cause, the boy was stung to compunction. " Sorry, Mum," he said, reverting to a schoolboy habit. " I don't mind you knowing. But it's not easy to talk. If I married her the governor would be certain to make hell about it. The daughter of his own shepherd, of all people. I know these self-made men."

" Don't bring your father into it," she advised him coldly. " Self-made or not, he may have good reason for opposing such a marriage."

" What reason ? "

Mrs Growcock countered his question with one of her own. " Don't you know what they say of her ? "

" What do they say ? " he asked.

" Well, for one thing, she's illegitimate. Did you know that ? "

Bert's face clouded, but lightened almost at once. " So that's it, is it ? All this fuss because Lottie's father wasn't married to her mother. That stuff's out of date, Mum. I know what I must do. I must get out of this and take a decent job. After all, I wasn't educated for farming."

"Farming paid for your education," she reminded him.

The talk was degenerating into a squabble, and both seemed powerless to arrest the degeneration. The son retired once more behind his paper; the mother resumed her knitting. But still his eyes scowled; and hers, staring absently at her work, were glazed with a vision of tragedy. "Are you very fond of her?" she asked softly, not looking up.

He grunted an embarrassed affirmative.

"How far has it gone?"

"Far enough." His voice choked. "There's no going back now, thank God!"

At that she looked up. "No!" she cried sharply. "Put the paper down, Bert, and listen to me. You must forget this girl, do you understand?"

He answered curtly, behind his paper: "I understand nothing of the sort. I shall marry her."

Her face was blanched with pain. Was this to be the bitter fruit of her long maternal labour, the carrying, the giving birth, the endless anxious vigilance? Was this the purpose of life, this crucifixion of the spirit? But, though she winced at her own agony, self-pity was lost in a larger and purer compassion. And in her deepest heart she found, as an ultimate refuge, pride like a rock. She was strong in despair. Life, whatever bitter turn it took, was a challenge that she scorned to decline : what it inflicted she would silently and disdainfully endure. But the heroic moment dwindled away.

"My darling boy," she began. A sound outside caught her attention, and the weakness in her snatched at the excuse. The door was flung open; her husband stood swaying in the doorway. "Oh, Bob," she said, "do come in. I want you to have a talk with Bert. We're in trouble."

But Bob Growcock was not in talkative mood. With an unmeaning grin, which passed instantly, he lurched towards the table and fell into a chair. In a few seconds he was asleep and snoring, with his head in a plate of bread and butter.

His son eyed him sardonically. "What price fetching swedes in the morning? I'll arrange the gentleman for bed, Mother. You be off!"

He went to shut the door his father had left open. He stepped out into the night, elaborately unconcerned and stubborn. A thousand stars struggled through mist. The moon was veiled in a menace that the grey wind voiced.

He stepped back into the house, shut and bolted the door, and returned to the kitchen, which his mother was just leaving. "Good night, Mum," he said, lightly kissing her forehead. "Dirty weather to-morrow, shouldn't wonder."

III

Harriet went to bed, to dream but not to sleep, or so it seemed to her. She did in fact

sleep a trifle of eight hours or so, but opening
her eyes in the darkness some long while before
dawn she felt that she had been awake all the
time, so faithful had been her dreams to the
glory that morning was to bring. She was alone
in the room. At Summers End, indeed, she was
altogether alone, her parents and her two mature
sisters being still at home. It was part of the
charm of Summers End that she did not belong
to it. With Uncle Bob and Aunt Polly she was
conscious of no sort of blood-relationship:
they were foreigners, strange and exciting in
everything they did. Nobody troubled her with
the information that Aunt Polly was her father's
eldest sister who had made an indiscreet runaway
match with a social inferior; nor would it have
been credible to her that her father could possess
a sister. Anyhow, an aunt is an aunt, and cannot
be a sister as well. In Harriet's world uncles and
aunts were as common as blackberries; everyone who became intimate with her family was
endowed with one or another of these titles,
which consequently had no definite meaning for
her.

Long before it was light she stole out of bed
to peep through the window at a world mysteriously dim and still. Bert's prediction had been
in part fulfilled; but the storm was now spent
and all the dark shapes outside were touched
with cold silver. It slanted across the gables
of the clustering outbuildings, flung a large, clear
triangle on the stable door, picked out the near

side of a gate-post, and settled, like quivering
tinsel, on the nose and forepaws of the hugest
dog in the world. At sight of this beast Harriet
could not repress a gasp. He seemed to be staring
with the most sinister intention straight up at her
window. She drew back into the shadow of the
room, only to find the object of her terror resolve
itself, under long scrutiny, into a tall bush. A
sloping field beyond, its surface broken by a
solitary haystack, lay as if tranced in sleep under
a shimmering diaphane of moonlight. Surely
it must soon be time for her to get up and go out
with Uncle Bob into that region of pale dream !
As she stood there, gazing out, gradually the
wonder of the waning night subdued her urgent
desire, so that she forgot it and was content to
float out on the wings of imagination and dip her
spirit in the dove-grey, luminous ocean. Night
paled under her stare.

The sudden apparition of a man in the yard
below, not unlike her uncle, startled her to a
realization of her vigil's purpose. The man led
out a horse and cart. He strode across the yard—
no mistaking that walk—and opened the gate
that gave on to the road. Tears rose to Harriet's
watching and incredulous eyes. Torn with
grief by her disappointment, she was affected
even more profoundly by this vision of human
infidelity. The stability of her world was
shaken, and she was afraid with a fear that had
never entered her heart before. When the
rumbling of the wagon had died away she turned

back, emptied of hope, to her bed. She felt herself deserted, forgotten, alone in a dark and alien universe.

In the morning, renewed by a subsequent sleep, she reduced Aunt Polly to confusion by an abrupt question. Even Bert paused in his break-fasting, surprised by the chill maturity of the child's tone. " Why did Uncle Bob go without me this morning ? "

" He must have forgotten," said Aunt Polly.

" I see."

Harriet's grave acceptance of the explanation was more eloquent than tears. Her simple affirmation seemed weighted with a significance of which she herself was unaware. It was as if she did indeed see, in clear-eyed despair, the incurable fickleness of mankind. It was as if sin and death suddenly confronted her. Bert, already tight-strung with suppressed emotion, could not bear to witness the change in her. " I tell you what," he impulsively said. " You come with me to the station with the milk. That'll be fun, eh ? "

Harriet, with her new sad wisdom, was half afraid to rejoice in this glorious prospect. " Ride in the cart with the milk-cans ! " she said, unable now to believe in such happiness.

" With the churns. Yes. Come along, or we'll miss the train."

Bert blushed, already, for reasons of his own, regretting his kindly impulse ; and, ashamed of his regret yet unable to stifle it, he

made shift to avoid looking at his cousin as
she ran out with him into the yard. For her the
world was born again in splendour. She forgot
her sadness and her brooding fears. Life once
more was friendly, caressing; and the fallen
sons of men were reinvested with the attributes
of deity. She stood first on one leg, then on the
other, twisting her slim body from side to side,
unable to rest; unable, in her impatience, to
take her usual delight in all the details of harness-
ing the grey pony; unable to fire at Bert the
customary round of excited questions about this
and that. If life held a purer joy than riding in a
cart in the company of huge milk-churns, she
was powerless to conceive it.

At last they were off. The road was slipping
away under the turning wheels. The churns
were rattling, and the milk in them audibly
splashing. It was evident now to Harriet that
she had been making a grave mistake about
Bert. He, and not Uncle Bob, was the nicest
person in the world. His gentleness when he
lifted her into the cart, his queer shy smile:
everything pointed to the same conclusion.
When she grew up she would come to live with
Cousin Bert for ever and ever.

"We'll stop here for a minute," said Bert,
pulling up. "Just have a look on the floor,
Harriet, to see if there are any earwigs about."
Harriet had advertised her opinion of earwigs.
"I won't be long."

Obligingly Harriet made a systematic search.

It was soon completed. She stood up to make her report. Where was Bert? "Cousin Bert-ee!" she called. But he was only a few yards away, in intimate talk with a young woman. Harriet caught sight of the pair just as they were making their farewells. The sight had no significance for her, and it was important that Bert's mind should be set at rest about the earwigs.

"There isn't any earwigs," cried Harriet. "Not even a little one."

Bert returned to her. His blush and his shining eyes, whatever their cause, made him look pleasanter than ever. "Is that your sister?" asked Harriet, in whose mind sisters and kisses were closely associated.

"Not exactly," mumbled Bert, with a smile. "Come, off we go again!"

But before the reluctant pony had decided to respond to his *clk-clk*, Bert became aware that an approaching wagon had stopped three yards ahead of him, and that in the wagon sat his father, regarding him from under black brows.

"Ho! ho!" roared Bob Growcock, suddenly assaulting the silence. "So that's the cause of your mopes, is it! That's why you wear a face like a thunderstorm! Bit o' wenching, *heigh?*"

Bert paled; the reins trembled in his hand. "Better mind what you're saying, Father," he said in a low tone.

"Mind what I'm saying, heigh? Ho, that's a good 'un. That's a real good 'un." The greenish eyes were screwed up in a kind of mirth, but Harriet no longer took pleasure in the spectacle. Her own eyes grew rounder and more frightened as she stared at this strange Uncle Bob. The man's mirth subsided abruptly. When he spoke again his voice had a new quality. "Well, who's the woman, lad?"

The question was peremptory, and the young man resented it. "That's my business."

"So 'tis," said Growcock, with irony. "Well, I never did! Now, if I might be guessing, she come out of yonder cottage, heigh?"

Bert's sullen silence answered him.

"I thought so." The man spat on his hands, and rubbed them together joyfully. "And that's Marsh's cottage. And the girl was young Lottie, heigh?"

"What if it was?" said Bert angrily. "I'm driving on."

Bob Growcock lifted his arms and suddenly bellowed with laughter. His mirth was gargantuan. His heavy frame shook, and his eyes dwindled to nothing. Bert stared in disgust, Harriet in rising fear. "By glory!" gasped the wild man, when he had gained some little control of himself, "that's the best joke I ever did hear. Good boy, good boy! Keeping it in the family, heigh?"

"What do you mean?" Bert's voice made Harriet turn to look into his face. She herself was trying to laugh, and wondering why Bert did not share in the joke.

"Ah, sonny, you don't know, do ye? Your fine schooling hasn't taught you everything. A rare fool I've got for a son. Lottie Marsh—that's a good 'un. Me own little girl! And you, you great booby . . .!" He gathered up the reins. "Son and darter, son and darter. It's a prime one."

Bert, with a jungle cry, slashed wildly out with the butt of his whip. His father's obscene laughter poisoned the sunlight. The whip fell harmlessly against the back of the other cart, which was already in motion. Diminishing peals of merriment continued to reach the boy's ears. His distracted glance fell on Harriet, who cowered white-faced in a corner, her arms hugging a churn as though it had power to comfort her. The sight shocked him back to his senses. Tenderness, reborn, overwhelmed him, bringing shame in its train. "Poor little dear!" he said, taking the child into his arms. "Did we frighten you?"

Harriet, understanding nothing but that he was no longer angry, quickly recovered; and at sight of her recovery, released from his duty, he abandoned himself to grief. He bowed his head and hid his face. For a long while he remained so, watched by the bewildered child. Harriet began to get weary of doing nothing, and so viewed with some relief the unexpected return of the strange young woman.

"Cousin Bert! Wake up, Cousin Bert! Here's the lady coming back."

He uncovered his face; seized the reins.

Harriet's mind reverted to her former question, which she remembered was still unanswered. "Is that lady your sister, Cousin Bert?" she asked again.

Bert Growcock raised his whip and administered a sharp cut to the dilatory and aged pony, who, surprised by this unwonted indignity, plunged forward. She trotted briskly, wondering what alien hand held her reins. The wheels flew round; the milk-churns rattled; and everything was jolly again.

From "The Baker's Cart"

PRENTICE

ONE is always running across them, these survivors of the dark age. They serve to remind one of the incredible fact that the war really did happen. It was in a public-house not too remote from Fleet Street that I met Jimmy Prentice again, all that was left of him. From his dark corner he stood eyeing me speculatively over the rim of his glass. He lacked an arm; and the livid scar that ran diagonally across his face, breaking the nose in two, lent him a sinister appearance. It was small wonder that I did not at first recognize him, and small wonder that as soon as I recalled his name there flashed into my mind a vision of George Leek. My last sight of Prentice had been at a Casualty Clearing Station behind Vimy. Then, his face had been swathed in bandages, his eyes shaded, his tortured body strapped to a bed. A whole man feels awkward in the presence of such disaster. What could one offer by way of consolation to a man permanently disfigured and disabled? Jimmy Prentice had no more than his share of vanity: that I knew well enough. But, when all is said, many of us would rather lose a limb than have our likeness destroyed. Disablement is disablement, and there's an end of it; but the face, be it plain or handsome, is one's very self, the living and outward sign of whatever lurks within, and its disfigurement involves, in some sense, a loss of identity. Prentice, therefore, was the victim of a double outrage ; and I was frankly afraid to learn how he was taking it.

" Here's a pal come to see you," said the medical orderly. To me he whispered : " Only two minutes."

" Well, Jimmy," said I, taking the plunge, " you've got a Blighty one this time, old cock."

For a few seconds he made no answer. Seeing his lips move, I bent over him.

" Who's there ? " said the grey lips.

I told him my name. " You remember me, don't you ? "

He grunted assent. " Bit dizzy, that's all. Yes, corp, I got a plateful all right. But nothing to what old George got. Old George Leek."

This was a dangerous subject. Prentice and Leek had been inseparable friends ever since I had known them. They came from the same street in Camberwell, but had never met there : a circumstance that not only drew them together but provided them with an inexhaustible subject for conversation and debate. They were for ever delightedly comparing notes about music-halls and cinemas they had both frequented and " tarts " they had both known ; and it seemed to them marvellous that with all they had in common they might never have become acquainted but for the war. " 'Spose you never come across a feller called Spink, George? 'Im what used to keep a lil paper-shop down the 'Igh Street? What, you knew 'im! Fency that now! You knew old Spink!" It seemed too good to be true that Leek had actually bought cigarettes from old Spink. To the bond of these common memories, which gave to Prentice and Leek an illusive grasp upon our vanished civilization, there was added, during the long alternation of action and so-called rest, the bond of incessant companionship. In the Rest Camp they pooled their wits against the Sergeant-Major, shamelessly dodging fatigues whenever they could; in the trenches they generally contrived to occupy the same dug-out. Once, once only, they went over the top together; more than once, squatting side by side, a shirt spread over each lap, they competed in the slaughter of lice. In this kind of tournament Prentice was generally the victor, though Leek ran him close enough to give a zest to the betting. They were an oddly assorted pair, and there was something correspondingly odd in their relationship. Prentice was—and is —a small, wiry fellow, whereas Leek had a biggish, clumsy body and a red moon face. Through Leek's composition ran a streak of singular simplicity, and, from the very first, little Prentice stood to him *in loco parentis*. Prentice, in fine, mothered Leek, as one might mother an awkward schoolboy: cheered him when he was down, steered him when he was drunk, and from motives purely sanitary kept

him away from brothels. All this, whether at
first or second hand, was common knowledge
in the platoon ; and it provided me with a good
reason for wishing to discourage further mention
of Leek. Jimmy Prentice had lost more than a
friend : he had lost his child.

" George caught it a lot worse than me,"
murmured the man on the bed, and seemed to
wait for my comment.

" I know," said I. " But your own little
packet'll see you home, Jimmy, well out of this.
That's what you've got to think of."

" Yes, I'm fixed up for duration. Not arf I
ain't." There was curiously little tone in his
words. " I'm a lucky one, corp, there's not a
doubt of it. But old George Leek—you oughter
seen old George and what they done to 'im,
corp. You ought, 'struth !' "

In point of fact I had seen George Leek, and
was busy trying to forget the sight. It had
confirmed me in the belief that war is an untidy
method of settling differences of opinion. I
felt a tide of sickness rising in me again, and so,
remembering the orderly's injunction, hastened
to make my farewells.

" Well, good luck, Jimmy. You'll be back
in Camberwell soon, you know."

It was a stupid blunder, as I realized the
moment it had passed my lips. I could not
shake hands with him ; I dared not so much as
lay a finger upon that immobile mass of pain.
A touch, had it been possible, would have

expressed more for me than my feeble speech, and I was exasperated to be denied it. Yet I was glad his eyes were masked when he said, still without tone, " No more Camberwell for old George."

II

These were the memories that stirred in my subconsciousness the other day when I caught sight of Jimmy Prentice flashing mute questions at me over his glass of bitter. I walked over to where he stood.

" I'm sure we've met before. Was it in France ? "

" Shouldn't wonder," he said, with a crooked grin. " Prentice, my name, sir."

" Of course ! " I remembered everything. " And mine——"

" Oh, I know *you* right enough," said Prentice, more at his ease. " I been lookin' at you this last *ten* minutes."

" Let's go and sit down—over there," I said. " We can talk in comfort."

We began drinking together and talking over old times. It was not at first very easy going. He began by being cursedly deferential, till I almost wished for another war that should get us back on the old, easy terms. But soon he thawed : told me what pension he got in consideration of his lost arm, and wondered whether the government would consent to take the other at the same price. My own contribu-

tions to the talk were somewhat halting, because
I could not get the idea of George Leek out of
my head and yet was afraid to introduce him
into the conversation. This obsession must have
made me appear absent-minded, and the consciousness of appearing so added to my embarrassment.

Over his fourth glass Prentice grew pensive.
" I 'spose," he said suddenly, " you wouldn't
remember that chap Leek I used to knock about
wiv : fat sort of feller wiv a red face ? "

" I remember him very well. He got knocked
out in the same scrap, didn't he ? "

" The same strarf," corrected Prentice.
" Crawling round on your belly and holding
what Jerry sent over. Not much scrap about
it. Georgie Leek, he was a fair knock-out for
getting into trouble. You din know 'im well,
did you, corp ? Not to *say* well ? "

" Only by sight," I admitted. " I know you
two were always together."

" You've got it," Prentice assured me.
" Always together we were. And need be,
what's more. Would you believe it, 'e come
from the same street as me, did George Leek,
and we never knew nuffin' of it till we got out
there. There was suthin' about George I
couldn't 'elp liking. 'E was like a blessed infant
in some ways, though never what you'd call a
fool, if you get me. And yet I dunno. One day
'e dragged me up out of a shell-'ole in the middle
of a big strarf, and you'd never guess what for.

''Ello, Jimmy,' he 'ollers down to me, ' you missin' a good thing down there, matey. Jest you kim up 'ere a minute.' Course, I tell 'im to go to 'ell, but in the end I 'ad to go up so as to make 'im take care of 'isself. ' Now you jest listen,' says George, cocking 'is 'ead a one side very sentimental. ' Why don't you take cover ? ' I asks him, mild as milk, but the least bit sarcastic. ' I've 'eard that 'ullyballoo before to-day.' But there wasn't no arguing wiv George. ' No,' says 'e. ' I din mean listen to Jerry. We've all 'eard *im*. Listen agin.' Then I 'eard what 'e mean—right up in the sky there was a bleed'n' lil skylark singing like one o'clock. It made me feel queer, but I din let on to George. ' Come to that, I've 'eard *that* before,' I tells 'im, pretty short. So I had, too, more'n once. But that was George all over. He was soft, there's no getting away from it. Did 'e ever tell you about 'is girl Ada ? ''

I shook my head, and Prentice launched at once into a long and highly circumstantial account of George's girl Ada. George had carried in his wallet six or seven photographs of Ada ; and Ada was nominated as sole beneficiary in the last Will and Testament that George had laboriously scrawled in the back of his paybook. Prentice could not deny that she was a pretty piece, but he would have it that she was not the girl for George. George, a hopeless romantic, was very much in love ; and Ada, it appeared, had neither difficulty nor compunction in playing ducks and drakes with him. It was George's trouble, Prentice told me, that he had never had anyone to look after him properly, and him a chap that needed more looking after than most. His own mother, for example, was nothing but an 'Oly Terror. Poor George had conceived the first and last passion of his life when he was a mere warehouse lad with I don't know how few shillings a week. Even that meagre wage, whatever it was, was pitilessly seized by his mother, and George provided with a minute fraction of it for his daily expenses, so that he was quite unable to pay Ada those little delicate attentions—cinemas and fish suppers—that courtship demands. But the time came when he got promotion, accompanied by an increase in salary of sixpence a week. This good fortune he determined to conceal from his mother. Thereafter, for ten consecutive weeks, he secreted a sixpenny-piece in the tail of his shirt. Then he made an appointment with Ada. For that great occasion, said Prentice, George got himself up regardless. He even went so far as to change into a clean shirt. Ada's disgust, when he confessed to having left his money behind, can be imagined, though I gathered from Prentice that she did not put George to the trouble of imagining it. The lover crawled home with his tail between his legs, and faced the second dose of music as best he could. By the fire stood his mother, a picture of wrath. On the mantelpiece, as his guilty eyes were

quick to see, was a neat little pile of sixpences,
" Come 'ere, yer cunning little bastard ! " cried
Mother. " Well, Mum," retorted George, with
more spirit than one would have given him
credit for, " *you* ought to know."

" And then," said Prentice, " she clouted 'im—
a feller, mind you, what could have squeezed
'er silly 'ead off wiv 'is finger and fumb. I'd like
to catch *my* muvver at sech tricks. But that,"
added Prentice, lapsing into his refrain, " that
was old George all over, soft, soft as pap. As for
that Ada, she was a dirty bit of goods and no
mistake. Cadgin' and crawlin' and naggin' 'im
all in once. Spendin' 'is rhino, and orf wiv other
chaps the same day. And did 'e ever learn
better ? Not 'im. You dunno George if you
think 'e learned better, corp. Leaf after leaf he
wasted runnin' round after that Ada, the lil
bitch ; and if ever he got so much as arf an
hour's 'and-'olding on the top of a bus 'e thought
'isself lucky. The things 'e used to tell me !
' You're a good boy, George,' she'd say to 'im,
laughing up 'er sleeve at 'im or my name's not
James Prentice ; ' there's no one I'd trust like
I trust you, George.' 'E din know the first
word about wimmin, and that's a fact, corp.
Used to make me fair mad to 'ear 'im. She
trusted 'im, did she ! When he tell me that I jest
up and tell '*im* suthin'. I tell 'im what she was
and what would do 'er good, and, bleeve me or
bleeve me not, 'e wouldn't speak to me for a
couple of days. Still, I din take offence. Can't

take offence wiv a soft bloke like that. Someone got to look after 'im, and me being from the same street, well, I took the job on, any old 'ow. Cleaned 'is buttons and 'elped 'im wiv 'is clobber when we was in barracks, and made 'im keep 'is 'ead down when we wasn't. And I 'ad to be sharp sometimes. 'Ad to pretend I thought the world of 'is girl Ada. When 'e got blotto down at a Base Camp this talk of Ada was the on'y thing 'ud keep 'im out of mischief. Course I got a bit short wiv 'im time and agin. I was sorry arterwards. ' Your girl Ada,' I tell 'im once, ' she'll be the deaf of me, George, and of you too, shouldn't wonder.' That's what I told 'im, corp, and I wasn't far out—about 'im, any'ow.''

Our glasses stood empty before us on the little round table at which we sat. Prentice declared that he had had enough. He refused my invitation to lunch, but agreed that a snack from the counter would do us both good. When I returned with a plate of sandwiches I asked him to explain in what sense Ada had been the death of George Leek. Whereupon he promptly withdrew his remark. He admitted generously that Ada couldn't help it, poor girl. If George chose to be such a noodle, well, it wasn't really her look-out. What he had meant was that if George hadn't been so soft about that girl, he might never have gone back to get them field-glasses.

"What field-glasses ? " I asked. " This is the first I've heard of them."

"It was," said Prentice, "like this here." The company, as I very well knew and no one better, had been holding a very exposed part of the front line. The relief was due in an hour and a half, but the enemy had got our position perfectly sighted and were sending over the best they had got. Their best proved very good indeed. When one in every ten of us had been suitably mutilated the order came through that we were to abandon the position. Its importance, we were led to understand, had been exaggerated, and the men that were to relieve us had been sent elsewhere. The retirement was orderly but hurried, and in the hurry George Leek left behind him a pair of field-glasses entrusted to his care by O.C. Lewis Guns.

"Blimey, said Leek, " I'm going back for them, Jimmy."

Prentice, who was slightly wounded, contented himself with a volley of oaths in disparagement of this suggestion. To carry it into effect involved crawling five hundred yards on one's belly into a shell-swept area.

"And me wallet, too," said Leek. "I've left me wallet behind, paybook and all."

At this Prentice took alarm. He knew, as well as Leek did, what was in that wallet. "Nah, George," he said urgently. "Stay where y'are, boy. No gal's worf it, let alone 'er photer."

But the ineffable George was already on his way. A few minutes later they heard, even above the shriek of artillery, a devastating human scream.

III

Prentice paused in his narration and stared for several seconds at the dregs in his glass.

He said presently : " Course, I oughta stopped 'im. But I wasn't quick enough, that's all about it, and I'd caught a lil packet in me thigh, what's more. Any'ow, when we 'eard that scream we 'ad to go and see about it. So me and another bloke—Evans, they called 'im—started orf. Oh yes, we got there all right. And we seen George Leek, not arf we didn't. Tell you straight, I never seen sech a sight. 'Ow 'e could scream at all wiv arf 'is face gorn beats me. But scream 'e did and never stopped a moment 'cep' to get 'is breaf back. Lyin' on 'is back all knocked to pieces, 'e was. Tell you straight, corp, I din like it. ' Come on, Evans,' says I. ' We got to get 'im out o' this.' So Evans takes 'old of 'is 'ead, and me 'is legs, and—Gawstruf, they twisted all ways ! Then George, old George Leek, 'e opened 'is eyes and seen me lookin' at 'im. And suddenly 'e stop 'is row and jest stared up at me. Looked at me sorta sick, as though I'd 'it 'im. Then 'is mouf moved, and 'e said, straight to me, wiv a sort of whistle in his voice, and a sorta sob : ' Jimmy . . . Crysake do us in ! ' Well, it was a fair knock-out. I dunno what to do. 'Im all to pieces like that and still alive. No getting 'im back. And whizz-bangs all round us —merry 'ell."

4

Prentice's voice wavered and was silent. I did not dare to look up, but presently I asked: " And what did you do ? "

" Well," said Prentice, slightly surprised by the question. " What could I do ? ' Crysake do us in ! ' says old George. So I out wiv me jack-knife and cut 'is bloody froat. 'E was a good pal to me."

The clock struck. It was three. The barman, who had already uttered several times his warning chant, " Time, gentlemen, please ! " now came to reinforce his persuasions. Prentice, before yielding up his glass, drank off the muddy dregs that from time to time during his narrative he had so sadly scrutinized. We got up and sauntered into the street, where, facing each other for a parting word or two, we heard the tavern key turn against us.

From " The Baker's Cart "

MISS LETTICE

NEEDING some stakes for my new fruit trees,
I called on Saunders, who knows everything, to ask him where they could be obtained.
Saunders is something more than a rector : he
is a shepherd of souls. He has an extraordinary
capacity for listening ; and listening, he tells me
(without any irony), is the most important of his
duties—far more important than preaching church
doctrine Sunday by Sunday. This is fortunate,
for in my belief Saunders's orthodoxy would not
survive a very minute scrutiny. The villagers
go to him with their most secret troubles, their
most lurid sins, and come away with hearts
eased, comforted by a platitude or two or by
wordless sympathy. His mind must be quite a
filing-cabinet of what are called human docu-
ments. With so much silent listening to do,
perhaps he finds me as useful as I find him
interesting ; for I am always willing, when he
is with me, to keep my ears open and my mouth
shut. He is a good talker but not a garrulous
one : it is the things he leaves unsaid, or half-
unsaid, that interest me most in his discourse.

As I had expected, he put me at once in the way
of getting my stakes. "Bowers, of Yew Tree
Farm, is the best man. He's a good fellow,

Bowers. For your own soul's sake you'll have to keep an eye on his charges : they're generally much too low. Yew Tree Farm—you know the place ? It's not really a farm at all : it's a ramshackle wooden house standing by the side of a timber-yard. Near poor Miss Lettice's cottage."

" Why do you call her poor ? " I asked. For Saunders was not in the habit of using that epithet without cause.

" Ah, haven't you heard ? She has been taken away, you know. You spend too much time among those books of yours, my friend. Why, it happened over a week ago. Pitiful affair. She lapsed suddenly into a kind of grotesque babyhood."

I can never hear of such an event without shuddering. " But she wasn't an aged woman ! " Already one spoke of her in the past tense as of the dead.

" She was fifty-eight," said Saunders ; and though genuinely shocked by the disaster I couldn't help being amused for a moment by the exactness of his information—it was so characteristic of him that he knew the woman's age to a year. " No," he added, " it wasn't the sort of thing that should happen in the ordinary course of nature."

" She had some shock," I suggested.

Saunders nodded. " The most cruel shock."

" And you no doubt were in her confidence," I insinuated.

Observing the curiosity that I tried politely

to dissemble, he looked at me for one silent moment and smiled. "There's no reason why you shouldn't know. You're a discreet fellow, and if you weren't such a misguided heretic I could find it in my heart to like you. Well, the cause of Miss Lettice's collapse was a psychological phenomenon that has a very old-fashioned name."

I waited for him to go on.

"A broken heart," said Saunders. "Miss Lettice is the victim of a hopeless passion."

"A hopeless passion," I protested, "at fifty-eight!"

Saunders drew his left hand from his jacket pocket and with it a pouchful of tobacco, which he tossed into my lap. "You're not in a hurry for ten minutes?"

I am never in a hurry when Saunders settles down into his chair with that air of pensive reminiscence; so, when we had both got our pipes going, he told me the story.

I

You are surprised (said Saunders) at being asked to associate Miss Lettice with the idea of passion, requited or unrequited. And, if you recall her small plump figure, and the nun-like pallor of the face that peered placidly from under her black bonnet, you will readily believe that hers was no ordinary passion. But it was passion: let there be no mistake about that;

I'm not going to fob off some remote mystical ecstasy upon you under that name. It's hard enough to credit that the heart of that staid, quaint, curtseying old spinster was aflame with a hunger that ultimately destroyed her, but the evidence is overwhelming. It is twofold, that evidence : there is the evidence of her words and the evidence of my own eyes.

My interest in Miss Lettice was first roused by a disquieting rumour that reached me, by a devious route, from a neighbour's wife who was employed by Miss Lettice to come in and do the rough housework for her. According to this rumour Miss Lettice was, for no stated reason, afraid of me. This puzzled me, as well it might, because at that time I didn't even know who she was : if we had met in the street I could not have recognized her. But it was more than puzzling : it was distressing. I knew that if I were to be of any use to the parish at all, fear was the very last emotion I must inspire. I examined the few sermons I had preached, for there, I thought, since they were the only communications I had had with the lady, the solution of my problem must lie. I looked for unsound doctrine, or for traces of hell-fire, or for anything else that could have alarmed a timid soul ; and I found nothing. You must remember that I was new to the job, and totally without experience, and altogether too disposed to take trifles seriously. To-day I should soon find a summary method of dealing with such a situa-

tion, but at that time it baffled me. I accepted
it for a while as a permanent minor discomfort.

I had promised myself to make friends, if I
could, with every member of my congregation,
and with as many others as I could contrive to
visit—no small undertaking in this wilderness of
scattered dwellings. Miss Lettice had to wait
her turn, of course, but it was a point of honour
with me that she should not have to wait beyond
it. Nervous, but also curious, I knocked at her
front door.

She received me, rather sternly, I thought,
but without discomposure. I was shown into
a tiny mottled room, which she called, I believe,
the parlour. It was rather crowded by furniture,
but the furniture itself was good and old and the
mantelpiece was laden with less than the usual
cottage assortment of bric-à-brac, though, of
course, there was the inevitable lustreware
glittering on each side of a marble clock, and,
equally inevitable, a pair of china dogs. The
pink beflowered walls were hung with very bad
pictures, in the Marcus Stone tradition, most of
them from Christmas annuals ; but there was not
a photograph to be seen anywhere. I remembered
having heard Miss Lettice described as " a real
lady in reduced circumstances," and I knew that
she supplemented a tiny inherited income by
giving music lessons.

For half an hour we talked of indifferent
things, and I began to fear that I should never
succeed in breaking through her armour of

frigid politeness. But in those days I was an obstinate young mule and determined to get at the truth behind that rumour. At last she gave me my chance.

"You have been in the parish three months, have you not, Mr Saunders?"

I chose to regard the remark as a challenge. "Three very busy months," I answered, loading my words with all the weight they would carry.

"Too busy, I'm sure, to visit middle-aged nobodies," she retorted. And then, taking sudden pity on my youthful confusion—I nearly twenty years her junior—she smiled in a way that seemed to betoken forgiveness.

It was a smile almost maternal, and it emboldened me. "Miss Lettice," I said, smiling in return, "why do you dislike me?" Placidly she shook her head. "Then why *did* you dislike me? Oh, never mind how I know. Things soon get about in a little community like ours."

She seemed startled. "What do you know?" Her eyes narrowed to gimlet points. The abrupt change in her manner disconcerted me. "What do you know?" she repeated defiantly, and, finding me silent, she flung another question at me, this time a veritable challenge: "Do you know about my son?"

Her son! So that was the cause of all the misunderstanding. "Nothing at all," I assured her. "Upon my word this is the first I've heard of him. Did you think . . ."

"Yes, I did. I thought you disapproved of

me, as your predecessor did, or maybe his wife.
I thought you were never going to call."

"But why," I protested, "why should I or
anyone presume to disapprove of you?" And
I wondered what travesty of religion had been
current in this parish before my coming.

She looked unaccountably severe. "I think
you don't understand."

"I think I do," said I, with cheerful arrogance.

"Mr Saunders, I am an unmarried woman,
and I have a son."

"Yes?" I said, simulating polite interest,
when in truth I was burning with curiosity.
But if I hoped to win her sympathy by this
unconventional attitude I was to be woefully disappointed. "You don't seem to realize the gravity
of what I tell you," Miss Lettice rebuked me. "It
is mistaken kindness to treat a sin so lightly."

"I want to be a friend to the parish, not a
judge." Priggish remarks rise readily to the
lips of a young man such as I was then. "Besides," I added, "if your son was a child of true
love there was no worse a sin than indiscretion."

But the confessed sinner would not hear of
such wickedness. "You, the vicar, to say a
thing like that! That's not the kind of teaching
we want in this parish. Why, I've done penance
all my life for that indiscretion, as you dare to
call it. I forfeited marriage and sent my lover
away. Not even for the child's sake would I con-
done our sin by marrying. And do you tell me
that all my bitter repentance was unnecessary?"

4*

What could I say? It would have been cruel to convince her that she had thrown away her happiness in sheer waste, sacrificed her life on the altar of a false god. I hadn't the heart to attempt it, so I fell back, I'm afraid, on Scriptural quotations, and left it at that. The familiar words seemed to comfort her and to reinstate me in her eyes as a moralist. None the less she was sufficiently assured of my sympathy to speak of her love, and as she spoke I began to wonder whether after all my pity had not been misplaced. Sin or no sin, the memory of her golden youth was dear to her. She was repentant enough, no doubt, when she remembered to be; but she did not live by morality alone. The woman in her still exulted, the woman's eyes still shone, in the knowledge that she had, however long ago, been found beautiful. "We were very young," she said, with disarming simplicity, "and we loved each other very much. He was all the world to me." Her cheeks flushed; her meagre bosom rose and fell tremulously—and in that moment I saw her as she had been, young, fresh, adorable, alight with limitless ecstasy, the incarnation of a man's desire. The transfigurement endured only for a flash, and flickered away, leaving me desolated with the stabbing poignancy of life. From that to this, I thought, we must all pass. To hide my emotion I led the talk back to her son. "And where is he now?" I asked. "Does he often come to see you?"

She smiled wanly. "He's all I've got. You

see there's a place set for him. You'll take a cup of tea with us ? "

The lid of the kettle that stood on the fire was already palpitating. Miss Lettice made the tea and enclosed the pot in a knitted cosy of green wool. For the next few minutes we exchanged only tea-table talk. But afterwards, when I made gestures of going, she confronted me wistfully, her eyes lit up once again. But this was a new light, and one more consonant with her years.

"Would you like to see his room ? " she said, almost in a whisper.

I expressed eagerness, and she led me to the threshold of a room so tiny that it made one think of a monastic cell. It was just large enough to contain a small single bed, ready for use, a wash-stand, and a miniature dressing-table. The furniture was all of childish dimensions. In the further corner, under the window, stood a cricket-bat. I glanced round with the vague smile of politeness. "So this is Bernard's room. A snug little place. And I see it's all ready for his return."

After a silence Miss Lettice sighed. "He would have been eighteen this coming April," she murmured.

I stared at her a moment in stupid wonder. "He would have been . . . do you mean . . . ? "

"He was stillborn," she confessed, and her glance dropped before my stare. "It was silly not to tell you at once. But Bernard's all I've got. He'd be a fine big fellow by now."

To avoid those glistening eyes I turned away, only to encounter a sight but one degree less pitiful : Bernard's cricket-bat—symbol of lusty young manhood, white flannels, sunlit turf— which no cricketer's hand had ever grasped. What could I say or do ? I was angered as well as touched by the wanton sentimentality of that room, and having murmured words of conventional comfort I hurried back to the vicarage. Not until many hours had passed did I succeed in hustling away my mood of melancholy ; and as I entered my own bachelor bedroom I shuddered to hear, in imagination, the good night uttered by that fond impossible woman to the ghost with whom she shared her home.

II

Saunders got out of his chair, as though the story were finished, and stood with his back to the fire warming the palms of his hands. There was a moment's silence, which I saw no reason for breaking, and then he began talking again. After that, he said, Miss Lettice and I were quite good friends. I became a constant and welcome visitor at her cottage : constant because her solitude was something of a pain to me, and welcome because she knew that to me she could talk about Bernard to her heart's content. And that, by Jove, was a privilege she lost no opportunity of exercising. How many times have I piously lied to that woman assuring her that my interest in her Bernard was insatiable! Often, as you'll readily understand, I was bored beyond expression, though I never lost my sense of the grotesque pathos of her life. But I must be careful not to let you suppose that she was a mere monomaniac. She knew, as well as I did, that she was playing a game of make-believe: she was not the victim of any sort of delusion, and her obsession never became pathological or threatened to become so.

Things went on like this for ten years or so. She lived untroubled among her dreams until some few months ago. During the war Bernard led an existence even more shadowy than usual. Of course he enlisted, and was wounded, and won decorations for his valour; and Miss Lettice, knitting socks for more substantial soldiers, continued to play her secret game by fancying that they would comfort the feet of her son. The change came, as I've said, not many months ago, and it showed itself first of all in our conversations. From those conversations Bernard was painlessly excluded, and his place taken by a young man weighing twelve stone or more. You'll know the name well enough—Jack Turnbull, the stationmaster's son. Jack began to loom so large in the hopes and fears of Miss Lettice that I became uneasy, the more so because I had been the instrument of bringing them together. It was this way. During the latter part of the war, and ever since, Miss Lettice had found it increasingly difficult to manage on her extremely modest income, and music pupils were more in request than ever. I did what I could for her by dropping a recommendation here and there, and among others I enlisted the active sympathy of old Turnbull. Together we hatched a little conspiracy, the upshot of which was that Jack, a big hulking fellow approaching thirty years, was fired with a sudden ambition to become an amateur pianist. Jack had done well in the army, and finding himself in mufti again, at a loose end, and with a captain's gratuity standing to his credit at Cox's, he lent himself very readily to the amiable fraud. His three hours' tuition a week was very useful to Miss Lettice; but it proved her undoing. For now we come to the hopeless passion I spoke of. And I needn't stop to assure you that there's nothing scandalous in this tragic affair. Miss Lettice fell in love with Jack, but the love she yearned to lavish on him was maternal love. If you think me perverse in calling that love a hopeless passion I must disagree with you. It was passion, and it was, in part, physical passion, as all human love must be. Why do we shrink from admitting that maternal love is as deeply rooted in the body as any other? Miss Lettice loved Jack Turnbull for his strength, his masculinity, his youth, and because, by a fatal coincidence, he was born in the same month of the same year as her Bernard. In a sense it was the calendar that killed the Miss Lettice we knew and set in her stead a witless child.

No doubt Jack seemed to her a gift from God, a wonderful consolation prize, a token of the heavenly forgiveness. Indeed, she told me as much when, with the air of imparting to me her dearest secret, she said that Jack was coming to lodge with her. She had bought some pretty things for his bedroom, worked ornamental bolster-slips with her own fingers, and replaced the dressing-table by a chest of drawers dragged in from her own room. I hardly dared to hint my misgiving. "Are you quite sure he is coming?" I ventured. "I fancied he would soon be looking out for a job. Young men can't remain idle for long nowadays, you know." But she wouldn't hear of my doubts. Jack would get work at the station under his father. He hadn't exactly promised to come to her, but she had urged it and she knew he would humour an old woman.

I was by no means so sure, and I made up my mind to tackle Master Jack at the earliest possible moment. I called at his father's house and left a message asking him to make a point, if he could, of calling at the vicarage. He came the same evening. "Well, Turnbull," I said, "I hear you're thinking of changing your quarters?"

He looked as guilty and uncomfortable as though I had surprised him with his hand in somebody's till. "Has it got round already? Why, I've told no one outside the family. Why can't people hold their tongues!"

"My dear fellow," I said. "I'm sorry if I've annoyed you. But I really don't see why you should be so secretive about it. And it wasn't your father who told me."

"Who was it?" He spoke curtly. Four years as an infantry officer hadn't improved his manners.

"It was Miss Lettice herself."

I have never seen a man more astonished. "Miss Lettice! Miss Lettice told you! Damn it, sir, she doesn't know!" After a moment's stupefied silence he added, with an air of apology, "But perhaps we're at cross-purposes. What was it that Miss Lettice told you?"

"Only that you're going to lodge in her house. Nothing to get excited about."

He began striding about the room. "We are certainly at cross-purposes all right. I thought you meant Canada. I'm leaving next week for Canada."

"For a holiday?" I ineptly inquired.

"For keeps," said Jack. "Mounted Police, with a commission soon, I hope. This country's gone to the dogs, sir."

Here was a pretty mess! "But look here, Turnbull, Miss Lettice has got it into her head that you're going there as a lodger. Have you given her any cause to believe such stuff?"

At that the swagger dropped off him. "That woman, I'm sorry for her, but she gets on my nerves. She gushes too much for my taste. She wants to mother me, if you ever heard such rot. And I won't be mothered."

"That's all very well," I cut in. "But why say this to me? Miss Lettice is the person you should complain to. Are you content to let her go on living in a fool's paradise?"

Well, you can pretty well guess how the conversation proceeded. We argued for the best part of three hours. Jack was determined not to yield to her devouring maternal affection, but he hadn't pluck enough to tell her so outright. He preferred to save his own feelings by equivocation. The coward does it with a kiss, you know, the brave man with the sword. But I must do him the justice to admit that, short of brutal explicitness, he did all he could to disabuse her mind of its fond fiction. I was aghast when I realized that the secret of his departure was being kept solely in order that he might slip out of the country without bidding her good-bye. After long battle I wrung from him a reluctant promise that he would spare her that culminating cruelty.

And that is the end of the story. I, too, was a coward, for I did not dare to visit Miss Lettice until Jack had gone. In point of fact I watched him off the premises and then stepped in, unwillingly enough, but hoping to afford the wretched woman some comfort, if only the comfort of distraction. The front door yielded to my push: it was seldom locked. I tapped at the door of the sitting-room. There was no sound from within. Gently I turned the handle and looked in.

" Good morning, Miss Lettice, " I said, with a cheerfulness that was idiotic, I dare say—but what was one to do ?

Miss Lettice sat staring at the wall in front of her, staring fixedly, motionless. Whether she heard my voice or not I don't know, but she neither moved nor spoke. I became very anxious and called to her again, offering such dry crumbs of comfort as came to hand. " Don't grieve, my dear Miss Lettice. There's still Bernard left to you." Something of that sort I said to her, but it made no difference at all. She was struck down, struck worse than dead, by the colossal and cruel power of love. And while I continued to stare at her with pity and horror, she slowly turned towards me, as though on a swivel, a face marred out of recognition by a smile. . . .

Saunders winced. His lips had hesitated in releasing those last words. Lifting one hand to his eyes, he turned away from me towards his bookshelves. There, with a book in his hand, he shrugged his shoulders as if to shake off the grip of a memory.

" If it's standard trees you're having," he remarked, " you'll want light six-feet stakes. Bowers is your man."

From " The Street of the Eye "

THE SUNFLOWERS

DUSK was falling. In a moment or two Aunt
Hester would call, standing, a black figure
of doom, in the kitchen doorway. Bedtime
yawned like the jaws of a dragon eager to appease
its appetite on a diet of little girls. Once in
bed, with the light out, you are in an enchanted
country, it is true. You have only to keep your
eyes tight shut to see pink mountains and purple
skies and golden rain falling, a world wrought in
bright dust, a heaving sea of many colours.
But enchantment is dangerous as well as exciting.
Those black ravines and the green catseyes that
puncture their blackness, those are less welcome.
And sometimes you feel yourself falling, falling,
into a dark void and out again, with all space,
all the queer dim colours of nothingness, spin-
ning round you. It is like the switchback at the
Crystal Palace, only much worse or much better,
as your luck determines. And soon your fancies,
if you fail to keep a firm grip on them, will get
quite out of control. They will stamp and chafe
and toss their manes, like a herd of zebras, and
whirl you away to the bottom of the deep pit of
sleep. At the bottom of the deep pit you must
lie, then, at the mercy of whatever dreams choose
to visit you. Angels of God, if Aunt Hester is

to be believed, have been deputed to keep watch and ward, angels specially trained for the protection of children from all night-fears; but, with so many bad bogies getting through the celestial cordon, one is forced to suppose that angels are not what they were in Aunt Hester's time: they, too, it would seem, have their sleepy moments, and discipline among them has been relaxed. Some of Sheila's dreams were so bad that she could not even speak of them, months afterwards, without tears welling up in her big dark eyes. Once she had dreamed that she saw two leering gentlemen, dressed like cricket umpires, emerge from her parents' bedroom carrying between them a bowl full of blood; she knew, in her dream, that these creatures had killed Father and Mother and now reigned in their stead, and she shuddered to see the hideous irony in their eyes as, with infinite care, they closed the bedroom door. A very long time ago that must have been; for Mother was but a memory now, a rather dim memory, dimmer by far than the terror of the dream itself.

So Sheila had better reason than most to fear bedtime. And to-night she had an additional reason. Three weeks or more ago her father had gone away (in search of Mother, perhaps), and now Sheila's ageing sorrow had been illuminated by an idea, an inspiration. She stood in the kitchen garden and gazed with ritual devotion upon the three feet of earth where her name was growing in letters of mustard and cress. This was now her sanctuary; this was one of the last works of her father's hand before that mysterious illness at the end of which, without saying good-bye, he had gone away. And she guessed that there was but little time left in which to effect her secret purpose.

Putting her hands together, she closed her eyes and whispered her prayer: "Dear God, will you please ask my father to come back, because Helena is very lonely and so am I." She waited confidently for God to answer her. He had spoken to people in the Bible; why shouldn't He speak to her? Struck by a sudden doubt, she went down on her knees and repeated her petition. Prayer uttered in an improper posture might never reach the divine ear at all, and, even if it did, might receive no attention. She waited for her answer. But the dusk gathered and no voice sounded, no vision appeared. The tall sunflowers, pursing up their faces for sleep, nodded near her, each peeping at her inquisitively (but not unkindly) with his single large brown eye. Intruders in the kitchen garden, great indolent creatures flaunting their flame in a region dedicated to utility, they yet seemed regally unaware of their intrusion. Uncle Peter had a fancy, which Sheila was glad to share, that a company of kings had missed their way home after an evening of revelry and had taken root, when the magic hour struck, by some sinister enchantment. To-night they seemed more than ever human, almost sympathetic, with no loss of their kingliness. Perhaps they, too, were eager for news of the vanished one.

No sign came from heaven. But there was yet hope. God might be busy listening to some-one else's prayers. He had so many people to attend to. But Jesus, who was specially the friend of little children, would surely answer her. To Jesus she therefore presented her new plea: "Please ask God to let my father come back again. My father's name is Mr Dyrle."

The silence remained, broken only by the minute sounds of eventide. Slowly, as Sheila waited, the petals of the sunflowers drooped closer together, like strange yellow eyelashes veiling velvet eyes. In those few moments the first two Persons of the Trinity were weighed in the balance and found wanting. Sheila re-solved that if the Holy Ghost proved more responsive she would never bother with the others again.

" Sheila ! "

A voice indeed, but not a voice from heaven. It was Aunt Hester calling her in to bed. Sheila lingered a while to give the Holy Ghost His chance.

" Coming, Auntie," she called. " O Holy Ghost, do be quick and answer ! "

" Sheila ! "—more insistently from Aunt Hester.

Sheila turned towards the house, her lip

trembling. Her cup of bitterness was full. With a sudden impulse of fear she ran down the gravel path to meet Aunt Hester. She hid her face in Aunt Hester's skirt, weeping.

"My dear child!" cried Aunt Hester, "what's the matter?"

The little girl spoke between sobs. "They're all too busy to listen, Auntie. I don't like Them a bit, do you?"

II

Next morning Sheila had forgotten her troubles. She had lain all night at the bottom of the dark pit, shut away from the external world, inside herself, secure from interruption. In waking life nothing entered the wonderland of her imagination but suffered transmutation into something rich and strange. In sleep, perhaps, the contents of her mind, her accumulated memories and imaginings, broke loose from control and paraded before her in a grotesque cavalcade. Of late heaven had interested her perhaps unduly, but only because her father had recently become a resident there. Normally, she was not a theological child. There was a time when she had supposed heaven to be only a greater and more glorious Crystal Palace (for with God all things are possible). Now, when she thought of it, it appeared to be a place very much like Penlington Gardens, with a large railway junction attached, a region where all lost friends, even dolls, would be found again.

She cherished the hope of finding even the Joneses there, notwithstanding their dinginess and their hatred of washing.

The Joneses had been Sydenham neighbours, but Sydenham, whence, with sister Helena and the invalid father, she had been transported by her father's cousin Hester (Sheila's aunt by courtesy), was already a fast-fading picture in her mind. From Hugo and Monica Jones she had caught a passion for keeping tadpoles in a jam-jar, and silkworms in a cardboard boot-box; but here, in the house at Penlington, such habits were discouraged. But Hugo and Monica were trifling losses to set against the great gains of Penlington. True, there was no front garden now, but there were iron railings, an iron gate, a series of broad stone steps leading to the front door, and a big hall; and, at the back, a small square garden enclosed by a wall. At the back, half a mile distant, was a junction of many railway lines. Sheila and the trains were great friends. The sound of them was seldom out of her ears. Sometimes at night she lay in bed listening to their gruff voices; sometimes she crept to the window to watch their lithe dark bodies, which sparkled with points of light. She wondered often whence they came and to what dark land they travelled. She tried to imagine who the people could be that went on these mysterious journeys. One traveller, she pretended, was a thin grey-bearded man who carried with him a glossy black bag like Father's;

but what that bag contained she could never quite decide.

Of comparatively pleasant things, such as these, Sheila may have dreamed during the night that followed her ineffectual prayer in triplicate. For in her experience it was the horridest dreams that could be remembered most clearly ; and on this particular morning she remembered none at all. She had also forgotten even her disappointment with the Holy Trinity, and consented to say her prayers as usual, convinced that she would not live through the day if she omitted them. There were still interesting things left in her world after all. She pretended this morning to be discovering it all for the first time. There was that winding stairway with its half-way landing from which through a window she could see fields like golden seas ablaze with buttercups. Not far from that window there was a tall yellow-faced clock with a very musical voice. He smiled at her when she passed him. Following the stairway, she came to the place where the banister rail curled round upon itself ; and so to the red-tiled hall. From the hall there was a choice of four ways : a small door admitting to the garden ; the drawing-room, a sombre place containing a walnut piano and filled with a strange Sabbath smell ; a long passage leading to the double bliss of the kitchen and the coalhouse ; and, lastly, the dining-room.

In the dining-room there was a wonderland known as Under-the-table, consisting mainly

of four fat mahogany table-legs and a thick
carpet with a pattern of blue, black, red and
yellow. She had great adventures on this carpet,
tracing out expeditions with her thumb and
pretending that the black was coal, the red fire,
and the yellow buttercup-fields or golden syrup,
by turns. In the contemplation of these delights
she lost account of Heaven's curious unrespon-
siveness to the petitions of little girls. In the
dining-room, too, were chairs with twisted legs
and with brown pads tied at four corners to their
hard seats ; and there was a black cupboard,
upon which, high and lifted up, dwelt a biscuit-
tin, decorated by the figure of a Chinaman.

While, after breakfast, she was rediscovering
these things, Uncle Peter rediscovered her.
Uncle Peter, whom she had known only three
weeks, was fond of describing himself as a sour
old bachelor of thirty-three. Since his return
from abroad some few months ago he had been
her greatest friend. He was very different from
his cousin, Aunt Hester, though she, too, was
rather nice. Uncle Peter was tall and had
a red face ; his wiry hair and bristly moustache
were flame-coloured ; and there were little
wrinkles round his often twinkling eyes. A
heavy gold chain stretched across his ample
waistcoat. His voice, and that only, was faintly
suggestive of the vanished Father.

"Hullo, She," said Uncle Peter. "What
shall we do to-day ? "

"Let's go to the gardens, Peter."

So to Penlington Gardens they went, that paradise of velvet lawns, of fountains, of weeping willows whose branches reached the ground and made little shut houses filled with green light, of drowsily humming insects, of bright tropical-seeming flowers, of orange trees growing in scented hot-houses, of little lakes and reeds and grassy banks. On the largest of the lakes lived real swans who would eat bread, and there was a big enclosure in which dwelt rabbits, with tiny white tufts of tails, in all their native wildness.

At noon Uncle Peter—that marvellous man— produced a packet of sandwiches. Sheila danced round him in rapture.

" Now we shan't have to go back to lunch, shall we ? "

" No fear," said Uncle Peter.

" While we have our sandwiches," said Sheila, " will you tell me a story ? . . . I'm not too big to be told stories, am I ? "

Uncle Peter looked judicial, pursing up his lips and cocking his head on one side.

" H'm ! Five, isn't it ? "

" Five and a half nearly," Sheila corrected him.

Uncle Peter looked grave. " Five and a *half !* Dear me ! "

Anxiously, round-eyed, she waited for his verdict.

" Do you think it's too old ? "

" Well," said Uncle Peter. " It *is* a great age, isn't it ? We must be careful, you know."

" Yes," agreed Sheila.

" But, then," cunningly added Uncle Peter, brightening a little, " we could keep the story-telling a secret, couldn't we ? "

" Oh, do you really think we could ? "

Mystery and guilt gleamed in Uncle Peter's eye. " Do you know, She, I believe I'll tell you a secret. Shall I ? "

" Please," she implored.

" Well, *I'm* thirty-three, and I'm often told stories."

She stared in wonder. " What—just like a little boy ? "

" Yes, you won't tell, will you ? "

" Of course not. . . . Will you tell me the story about the boy who had a penknife, please, Peter ? "

There were at least three kinds of stories. There were the quite true Sunday stories like Joseph and the Coat of Many Colours—favourites, these, of Aunt Hester's ; there were fairy-tales which were very nearly true ; and there were doubtful ones with morals. The Boy and the Penknife was Uncle Peter's own, and unique in being the only perfectly true story outside the Bible. It was about a boy whose mother gave him three pennies.

" What did she do that for ? " asked Sheila.

" Because he never interrupted her stories, I fancy," said Uncle Peter rather woefully. " Well, as soon as he had got his pennies he ran off . . ."

" Didn't he——" began Sheila.

". . . after thanking his mother, of course," said Uncle Peter hastily. " Ran off to look in a shop-window where there was a fine penknife he wanted."

" A pearl one," Sheila murmured.

" So he went in and bought it."

" Yes, but first——"

" Oh, first he put his nose against the window-pane and gazed . . ."

" Until his nose got quite cold," supplemented Sheila. " It did last time, you know."

" Quite right. Then, when he had bought it, he went to the river-side to cut bulrushes. All of a sudden . . ."

At this point in the narration Sheila began to feel very uneasy. There was, she knew, tragedy coming ; a queer feeling was in her throat ; but she was determined not to spoil the story by remembering what came next.

" Did he fall in ? " she asked.

" No," said Uncle Peter. " He nearly fell in, but not quite. But all of a sudden "—the listener held her breath—" his hand slipped and the knife sank to the bottom of the river."

Sheila sat in wistful silence, her large eyes imploring the story-teller not to pause too long there. Her lip quivered in a way that made Uncle Peter hastily continue.

" But he didn't cry, this boy. Not he ! And in time he grew to be a man."

" Is it anyone I know ? " asked Sheila, all innocence.

Gravely he nodded.

" The postman ? "

" No."

" The hairy man next door ? "

" You mean our handsome neighbour with the brown beard, no doubt. No, it isn't him."

" Who is it, Uncle Peter ? "

" I am the man," said Uncle Peter.

" *You !* " cried Sheila in astonishment. The same revelation had astonished her only a few days before.

" The very identical," said Uncle Peter.

" What's that ? "

" Have another sandwich," replied Uncle Peter.

III

At tea-time, back in the house at Penlington, she confided to Aunt Hester in an unguarded moment of enthusiasm that they had seen a fairy.

" He was bathing in a buttercup," added Sheila.

Aunt Hester held up an admonitory forefinger. " Little girls mustn't tell stories."

" My dear Hester ! " cried Uncle Peter. His voice was infinitely weary, and its weariness seemed to lash poor Hester cruelly. She met his glance in dumb distress, as though he had whipped her, and then she turned her head away to look fixedly out of the window. Her lip trembled.

Aunt Hester was like that. A word from

Uncle Peter would always subdue her. Sheila, staring with all her eyes, was frightened by the expectation of seeing Aunt Hester burst into tears. But the disaster was averted. "Get on with your tea, darling," said Aunt Hester gently, and the little girl, bending again over her plate, pondered the mystery of these two familiar yet remote creatures, between whom there existed a something that altogether transcended her understanding. By what virtue did Peter, that harmless and so friendly old gentleman of thirty-three, exercise careless dominion over his prim cousin Hester? Sheila recalled, as she bit a half-moon out of her slice of bread and butter, how it was at Peter's wish that the sunflowers had been suffered to remain in the kitchen-garden usurping space that belonged by right to more useful vegetation. Aunt Hester had said they must be dug up and transplanted. "Oh, let them stay, my dear," Uncle Peter had exclaimed. "They're so delightfully discordant." And Aunt Hester had blushed prettily : Sheila couldn't guess why.

Sheila was in a hurry to get down from table. But she dared not ask permission, because to-day there was an alien presence among them. Upstairs there lived an inconceivably ancient woman known as Granny. She lived in a huge chair, her feet on a hassock, at her side a spittoon, within her reach a bell-rope. She wore a black pleated bodice and a white cap. Her white and withered frailty was terrifying, so easily might her large face fall to pieces like an incandescent gas-mantle. She sat all day sipping peppermint, smelling salts from a bottle, making little grunting noises, opening and shutting (with a strange popping sound) her spectacle-case. And for hours she would hold close to her dim eyes her Book of Common Prayer and make pretence of reading the collect for the day. Seldom, indeed, did she descend from the Olympus to which her inhuman agedness entitled her, but whenever she did so it was to Sheila as if some colossal and indifferent deity had come amongst them. Most often these descents were made on behalf of visitors. Granny would make the perilous journey, assisted by her two grandchildren, in order to prove herself still queen of the household.

Inscrutable caprice had brought Granny to the tea-table to-day, and Sheila therefore itched for freedom. When at last she did escape she ran off to Camelot, the beautiful brickfield that backed on to the garden. This was forbidden ground, for Sheila was permitted to visit Camelot only in the company of the Madders girls, the eldest of whom had given the place its name. But for the moment she forgot the prohibition. At first she thought she would take Lady Betty with her for a treat, but a moment later that plan was abandoned. Lady Betty had recently been guilty of several acts of disobedience. She had resolutely refused to be fed; she had knocked her medicine out of Sheila's hand; and she had coughed shamelessly without attempting to turn her head away first. These things could not pass unpunished. Without proper discipline Sheila's large family of dolls—for were there not also Millicent and Agnes and Sammy the little black boy?—could never be brought up successfully. So Lady Betty, despite her tears (" And that's more than half temper, too ! " said Sheila), was left behind without ruth.

Camelot was an agreeable refuge. Sheila lay among the tall grasses and watched the insects running busily about their little world : ants going a-marketing, spiders that seemed to fly over the ground, so quickly did they move, and a red soldier who sometimes climbed up grass-blades and sat on the top of what must have been to him tall trees. Sheila followed the adventures of this brave soldier for a long while, saw with sympathy how he met and surmounted all the obstacles in his path. She wondered whether it was his mother who had made him his red coat, and whether she was very angry with him when he returned home from his rambles with torn clothes. After a while he disappeared under the grass and she saw him no more. A big dock-flower near by was nodding its head towards her, whispering something, she knew, but what she could not quite decide. She rather thought it was telling her a fairy-tale : of how in that little world of grass there dwelt a king who had a crown made of moss, and robes of thistledown, and who held his court under a toadstool. He had three sons, this king, and one day he said to them : " Whichever of you kills the lady-toad that sits day and night upon this stool, for him I will build the finest palace in the world. It shall be made of chocolate cream, and there will be cherries growing in the garden all the year round. And whoever lives in it needn't ever go to bed till nine o'clock." So the eldest son said : " I'm the fellow for that job, being the eldest of your sons. The second is too fat, and the youngest only a baby." But when he climbed, sword in hand, upon the neighbouring daisy and saw the big ugly toad squatting on that toadstool glaring about her, he was frightened and ran away. Then the second son said to his father, the king : " I knew all along he would muff it. You watch me." And off he went to the twine-shop kept by a grass-hopper to buy some twine to tie the toad up with. While he was making these preparations, the third son, who wasn't a baby at all, climbed on to the toadstool. " Good morning ! " said he to the lady-toad, " how are you ? " " Nicely," replied the toad, " hoping you are the same as it leaves me at present. You're the king's son, aren't you ? " " Yes," said the king's son, " and I've come to kill you." " Thank you very much," croaked the old toad. " Kill away !" But when the king's son whipped out his sword and stuck it into the toad, she changed into a beautiful princess. And the young prince married her and they lived happily ever after in the finest palace in the world which the king with his own hands had built for them.

This was the tale the dock-flower told, as it nodded its head to Sheila and rocked to and fro.

"But that's one of Peter's tales," said Sheila to the dock-flower. "You know very well it is."

The dock-flower, convicted of piracy, very wisely abstained from reply. But Sheila noticed that it had an ashamed look, very much the kind of look that Lady Betty always had when caught in the act of putting her fingers in the tea-cup.

Sheila was distracted by a little wailing cry. Something soft rubbed against her cheek, a fluffy ball of life, a stray kitten. "Oh, you darling!" cried Sheila. She hugged the creature close and jumped to her feet. The world of beautiful pretence faded like the merest dream. This was real; this was warm and breathing. She ran homeward a few steps and then paused again to examine with ecstasy this new and most wonderful treasure. The kitten's warm purring softness sent little shudders of delight running over her body. "It's alive," she whispered to herself. "It's alive!" Quite unexpectedly there flashed into her mind a vision of Aunt Hester's hungry eyes and trembling lips; and now in a vague dim way she understood something of their meaning. Tears for Aunt Hester quivered on her long lashes.

IV

The kitten was a great success. Even Sheila's truancy was forgotten in the excitement of greeting this new member of the household. For no one dared to doubt, in the face of Sheila's delight, that the kitten had come to stay. The enthusiasm with which it lapped up a saucerful of milk moved Aunt Hester to declare that the poor little thing was starving, and she was eager to accept its prettiness as an earnest of good behaviour. Sheila, in spite of protests both from Aunt Hester and from the kitten itself, insisted on sprinkling a few drops of water on the creature's nose in witness of the fact that it was to be known henceforward as Tommy. Uncle Peter promised to provide two pennyworth of catsmeat as a christening gift.

Having watched the kitten's antics for five minutes, Uncle Peter remarked that he wouldn't be back to supper.

Hester's happiness evaporated visibly. Her face became a mask. "Very well, Peter," she said, in a dull tone. "You have your key, I expect."

"Yes, thanks." Uncle Peter was desperately cheerful. "Wouldn't do to forget that and have to knock you all up, hey!" He tried to be amused by the idea. "Well, so long!" he said, pausing at the door.

Going to bed was a dismal affair after so much excitement, chiefly because Aunt Hester was preoccupied with thoughts of her own. "God bless Granny and Aunt Hester and Uncle Peter and Father and Tommy and me and make me a good girl, Amen," said Sheila, running her words into one enormous polysyllable; and Aunt Hester, the overseer of prayer, did not rebuke her for her unseemly speed.

"Isn't he a dear!" said Sheila, in a last attempt to make conversation before the candle was blown out. "Don't *you* think he's a dear, Auntie?"

V

Next morning, at breakfast, Uncle Peter seemed at once shamefaced and happy. As for Aunt Hester, she kept up a creditable show of gaiety. "When are you going to tell Granny?" she asked him.

Peter blushed. "Oh, I don't know," he said, in an offhand way. "*You* tell her, Hester."

"Very well." Hester smiled. "Sheila and I will tell her after breakfast. You'll be busy to-day, I expect?"

"Bit of shopping," he confessed, with the air of one caught with his hand in somebody's till.

"Ah, I thought so."

So, when Uncle Peter had run off to catch the ten-eighteen for town, Hester and Sheila went hand-in-hand to knock at Granny's door. The knock was the merest formality, a hollow ritual, for Granny seldom heard knocks at the door and never, even if she heard them, responded. Having knocked, they entered timidly, Sheila trying to hide behind Hester's skirts.

" Some news for you, Granny."

" Eh ? " queried the old woman.

" News for you, Granny."

" I'm too old for news, my child. . . . There, don't stand like a great baby, keeping me in suspense. If he's dead tell me so at once, and be off with you. I shall be the next to go. Poor Peter, he never was a strong lad."

" No one's dead. It's good news. About Peter."

She imparted her good news about Peter.

" Eh ! " muttered Granny. " Nonsense ! He's only a boy ! "

" Aren't you pleased, Granny ? "

" What a tale ! " sniffed the ancient, scornfully. " When is my glass of milk coming, Hester ? "

The glass of milk provided, Aunt Hester, on whom a strange silence had fallen, wandered into the garden still gripping Sheila's hand. They walked up and down the gravel paths, gravely meditating, and finally, at Sheila's request, they entered the kitchen-garden to pay homage to the kingly sunflowers. At sight of them Aunt Hester became rigid, a woman of stone. " Fetch me the garden scissors, dear. They're in the tool-shed."

Sheila ran willingly to do her aunt's bidding. But the scissors were hard to find, and she returned to Hester's side just in time to see the last of the sunflowers fall. Flaming yellow, the disenchanted kings drooped upon the earth, riven from their roots.

"I shan't want the scissors now, darling. . . . How sticky my fingers are!"

Torn between wonder and grief, Sheila stared up into her companion's face, trying to read the dark enigma written there. "But Uncle Peter said they should stay," she wailed.

"I dare say. But he won't mind now. He's going away from us soon to be married."

Light, dim but unmistakable, dawned in Sheila's mind. "Never mind, Auntie," she said, with a gush of compassion. "I'll give you my Tommy if you like."

Aunt Hester turned away quickly, and ran into the house.

From "The Baker's Cart"

DEARTH'S FARM

I<small>T</small> is really not far : our fast train does it in eighty minutes. But so sequestered is the little valley in which I have made my solitary home that I never go to town without the delicious sensation of poising my hand over a lucky-bag full of old memories. In the train I amuse myself by summoning up some of those ghosts of the past, a past not distant, but sufficiently remote in atmosphere from my present to be invested with a certain sentimental glamour. "Perhaps I shall meet you—or you." But never yet have I succeeded in guessing what London held up her sleeve for me. She has that happiest of tricks—without which paradise will be dull indeed—the trick of surprise. In London, if in no other place, it is the unexpected that happens. For me Fleet Street is the scene *par excellence* of these adventurous encounters, and it was in Fleet Street, three months ago, that I ran across Bailey, of Queens', whom I hadn't seen for five years. Bailey is not his name, nor Queens' his college, but these names will serve to reveal what is germane to my purpose and to conceal the rest.

His recognition of me was instant ; mine of him more slow. He told me his name twice ;

we stared at each other, and I struggled to disguise the blankness of my memory. The situation became awkward. I was the more embarrassed because I feared lest he should too odiously misinterpret my non-recognition of him, for the man was shabby and unshaven enough to be suspicious of an intentional slight. Bailey, Bailey . . . now who the devil was Bailey? And then, when he had already made a gesture of moving on, memory stirred to activity.

" Of course, I remember. Bailey. Theosophy. You used to talk to me about theosophy, didn't you? I remember perfectly now." I glanced at my watch. " If you're not busy let's go and have tea somewhere."

He smiled, with a hint of irony in his eyes, as he answered : " I'm not busy." I received the uncomfortable impression that he was hungry and with no ordinary hunger, and the idea kept me silent, like an awkward schoolboy, while we walked together to a teashop that I knew.

Seated on opposite sides of the tea-table we took stock of each other. He was thin, and his hair greying ; his complexion had a soiled unhealthy appearance ; the cheeks had sunk in a little, throwing into prominence the high cheekbones above which his sensitive eyes glittered with a new light, a light not of heaven. Compared with the Bailey I now remembered so well, a rather sleek young man with an almost feline love of luxury blossoming like a tropical plant in the exotic atmosphere of his Cambridge

5*

rooms, compared with that man this was but a pale wraith. In those days he had been a flaming personality, suited well—too well, for my plain taste—to the highly coloured orientalism that he affected in his mural decorations. And co-existent in him with this lust for soft cushions and chromatic orgies, which repelled me, there was an imagination that attracted me : an imagination delighting in highly coloured metaphysical theories of the universe. These theories, which were as fantastic as *The Arabian Nights*, and perhaps as unreal, proved his academic undoing : he came down badly in his Tripos, and had to leave without a degree. Many a man has done that and yet prospered, but Bailey, it was apparent, hadn't prospered. I made the conventional inquiries, adding, " It must be six or seven years since we met last."

" More than that," said Bailey morosely, and lapsed into silence. " Look here," he burst out suddenly, " I'm going to behave like a cad. I'm going to ask you to lend me a pound note. And don't expect it back in a hurry."

We both winced a little as the note changed hands. " You've had bad luck," I remarked, without, I hope, a hint of pity in my voice. " What's wrong ? "

He eyed me over the rim of his teacup. " I look a lot older to you, I expect ? "

" You don't look very fit," I conceded.

" No, I don't." His cup came down with a nervous slam upon the saucer. " Going grey, too, aren't I?" I was forced to nod agreement. "Yet, do you know, a month ago there wasn't a grey hair in my head. You write stories, don't you? I saw your name somewhere. I wonder if you could write my story. You may get your money back after all. . . . By God, that would be funny, wouldn't it!"

I couldn't see the joke, but I was curious about his story. And after we had lit our cigarettes he told it to me, to the accompaniment of a driving storm of rain that tapped like a thousand idiot fingers upon the plate-glass windows of the shop.

II

A few weeks ago, said Bailey, I was staying at the house of a cousin of mine. I never liked the woman, but I wanted free board and lodging, and hunger soon blunts the edge of one's delicacy. She's at least ten years my senior, and all I could remember of her was that she had bullied me when I was a child into learning to read. Ten years ago she married a man named Dearth— James Dearth, the resident owner of a smallish farm in Norfolk, not far from the coast. All her relatives opposed the marriage. Relatives always do. If people waited for the approval of relatives before marrying, the world would be depopulated in a generation. This time it was religion. My cousin's people were primitive and methodical in their religion, as the name of their sect confessed ; whereas Dearth professed a universal toleration that they thought could only be a cloak for indifference. I have my own opinion about that, but it doesn't matter now. When I met the man I forgot all about religion : I was simply repelled by the notion of any woman marrying so odd a being. Rather small in build, he possessed the longest and narrowest face I have ever seen on a man of his size. His eyes were set exceptionally wide apart, and the nose, culminating in large nostrils, made so slight an angle with the rest of the face that seen in profile it was scarcely human. Perhaps I exaggerate a little, but I know no other way of explaining the peculiar revulsion he inspired in me. He met me at the station in his dogcart, and wheezed a greeting at me. " You're Mr Bailey, aren't you ? I hope you've had an agreeable journey. Monica will be delighted." This seemed friendly enough, and my host's conversation during that eight-mile drive did much to make me forget my first distaste of his person. He was evidently a man of wide reading, and he had a habit of polite deference that was extremely flattering, especially to me who had had more than my share of the other thing. I was cashiered during the war, you know. Never mind why. Whenever he laughed, which was not seldom, he exhibited a mouthful of very large regular teeth.

Dearth's Farm, to give it the local name, is a place with a personality of its own. Perhaps every place has that. Sometimes I fancy that the earth itself is a personality, or a community of souls locked fast in a dream from which at any moment they may awake, like volcanoes, into violent action. Anyhow, Dearth's Farm struck me as being peculiarly personal, because I found it impossible not to regard its climatic changes as changes of mood. You remember my theory that chemical action is only psychical action seen from without? Well, I'm inclined to think in just the same way of every manifestation of natural energy. But you don't want to hear about my fancies. The farmhouse, which is approached by a narrow winding lane from the main road, stands high up in a kind of shallow basin of land, a few acres ploughed, but mostly grass. The country-side has a gentle prettiness more characteristic of the south-eastern counties. On three sides wooded hills slope gradually to the horizon; on the fourth side grassland rises a little for twenty yards and then curves abruptly down. To look through the windows that give out upon this fourth side is to have the sensation of being on the edge of a steep cliff, or at the end of the world. On a still day, when the sun is shining, the place has a languid beauty, an afternoon atmosphere. You remember Tennyson's Lotus Isles, "in which it seemed always afternoon": Dearth's Farm has something of that flavour on a still day. But such days are rare; the two or three I experienced shine like jewels in the memory. Most often that stretch of fifty or sixty acres is a gathering-ground for all the bleak winds of the earth. They seem to come simultaneously from the land and from the sea, which is six miles away, and they swirl round in that shallow basin of earth, as I have called it, like maddened devils seeking escape from a trap. When the storms were at their worst I used to feel as though I were perched insecurely on a gigantic saucer held a hundred miles above the earth. But I am not a courageous person. Monica, my cousin, found no fault with the winds. She had other fears, and I had not been with her three days before she began to confide them to me. Her overtures were as surprising as they were unwelcome, for that she was not a confiding person by nature I was certain. Her manners were reserved to the point of diffidence, and we had nothing in common save a detestation of the family from which we had both sprung. I suppose you will want to know something of her looks. She was a tall, full-figured woman, handsome for her years, with jet-black hair, a sensitive face, and a complexion almost Southern in its dark colouring. I love beauty and I found pleasure in her mere presence, which did something to lighten for me the gloom that pervaded the house ; but my pleasure was innocent enough, and Dearth's watchdog airs only amused me. Monica's eyes—unfathomable pools—seemed troubled whenever they rested on me : whether by fear or by some other emotion I didn't at first know.

She chose her moment well, coming to me

when Dearth was out of the house, looking after
his men, and I, pleading a headache, had refused
to accompany him. The malady was purely
fictitious, but I was bored with the fellow's
company, and sick of being dragged at his heels
like a dog for no better reason than his too evident jealousy afforded.

"I want to ask a kindness of you," she said.
"Will you promise to answer me quite frankly?"
I wondered what the deuce was coming, but I
promised, seeing no way out of it. "I want
you to tell me," she went on, "whether you see
anything queer about me, about my behaviour?
Do I say or do anything that seems to you odd?"

Her perturbation was so great that I smiled
to hide my perception of it. I answered jocularly:
"Nothing at all odd, my dear Monica, except
this question of yours. What makes you ask
it?"

But she was not to be shaken so easily out of
her fears, whatever they were. "And do you
find nothing strange about this household
either?"

"Nothing strange at all," I assured her.
"Your marriage is an unhappy one, but so are
thousands of others. Nothing strange about
that."

"What about him?" she said. And her eyes
seemed to probe for an answer.

I shrugged my shoulders. "Are you asking
for my opinion of your husband? A delicate
thing to discuss."

143

"We're speaking in confidence, aren't we!"
She spoke impatiently, waving my politeness
away.

"Well, since you ask, I don't like him. I
don't like his face: it's a parody on mankind.
And I can't understand why you threw yourself
away on him."

She was eager to explain. "He wasn't
always like this. He was a gifted man, with
brains and an imagination. He still is, for all I
know. You spoke of his face—now how would
you describe his face, in one word?"

I couldn't help being tickled by the comedy
of the situation: a man and a woman sitting
in solemn conclave seeking a word by which
to describe another man's face, and that man her
husband. But her air of tragedy, though I
thought it ridiculous, sobered me. I pondered
her question for a while, recalling to my mind's
eye the long narrow physiognomy and the
large teeth of Dearth.

At last I ventured the word I had tried to
avoid. "Equine," I suggested.

"Ah!" There was a world of relief in her
voice. "You've seen it, too."

She told me a queer tale. Dearth, it appears,
had a love and understanding of horses that was
quite unparalleled. His wife, too, had loved
horses and it had once pleased her to see her
husband's astonishing power over the creatures,
a power which he exercised always for their
good. But his benefactions to the equine race

were made at a hideous cost to himself of which he was utterly unaware. Monica's theory was too fantastic even for me to swallow, and I, as you know, have a good stomach for fantasy. You will have already guessed what it was. Dearth was growing, by a process too gradual and subtle for perception, into the likeness of the horses with whom he had so complete sympathy. This was Mrs Dearth's notion of what was happening to her husband. And she pointed out something significant that had escaped my notice. She pointed out that the difference between him and the next man was not altogether, or even mainly, a physical difference. In effect she said : " If you scrutinize the features more carefully, you will find them to be far less extraordinary than you now suppose. The poison is not in his features. It is in the psychical atmosphere he carries about with him : something which infects you with the idea of horses and makes you impose that idea on his appearance, magnifying his facial peculiarities." Just now I mentioned that in the early days of her marriage Monica had shared this love of horses. Later, of course, she came to detest them only one degree less than she detested her husband. That is saying much. Only a few months before my visit matters had come to a crisis between the two. Without giving any definite reason, she had confessed, under pressure, that he was unspeakably offensive to her ; and since then they had met only at meals and always reluctantly.

She shuddered to recall that interview, and I shuddered to imagine it. I was no longer surprised that she had begun to entertain doubts of her own sanity.

But this wasn't the worst. The worst was Dandy, the white horse. I found it difficult to understand why a white horse should alarm her, and I began to suspect that the nervous strain she had undergone was making her inclined to magnify trifles. "It's his favourite horse," she said. "That's as much as saying that he dotes on it to a degree that is unhuman. It never does any work. It just roams the fields by day, and at night sleeps in the stable." Even this didn't, to my mind, seem a very terrible indictment. If the man was mad on horses, what more natural than this petting of a particular favourite?—a fine animal, too, as Monica herself admitted. "Roams the fields," cried my poor cousin urgently. "Or did until these last few weeks. Lately it has been kept in its stable, day in, day out, eating its head off and working up energy enough to kill us all." This sounded to me like the language of hysteria, but I waited for what was to follow. "The day you came, did you notice how pale I looked? I had had a fright. As I was crossing the yard with a pail of separated milk for the calves, that beast broke loose from the stable and sprang at me. Yes, Dandy. He was in a fury. His eyes burned with ferocity. I dodged him by a miracle, dropped the pail, and ran back to the house shrieking for

146

help. When I entered the living-room my husband feigned to be waking out of sleep. He didn't seem interested in my story, and I'm convinced that he had planned the whole thing." It was past my understanding how Dearth could have made his horse spring out of his stable and make a murderous attack upon a particular woman, and I said so. " You don't know him yet," retorted Monica. " And you don't know Dandy. Go and look at the beast. Go now, while James is out."

The farmyard, with its pool of water covered in green slime, its manure and sodden straw, and its smell of pigs, was a place that seldom failed to offend me. But on this occasion I picked my way across the cobblestones thinking of nothing at all but the homicidal horse that I was about to spy upon. I have said before that I'm not a courageous man, and you'll understand that I stepped warily as I neared the stable. I saw that the lower of the two doors was made fast and with the more confidence unlatched the other.

I peered in. The great horse stood, bolt upright but apparently in a profound sleep. It was, indeed, a fine creature, with no spot or shadow, so far as I could discern, to mar its glossy whiteness. I stood there staring and brooding for several minutes, wondering if both Monica and I were the victims of some astounding hallucination. I had no fear at all of Dandy, after having seen him ; and it didn't alarm me when, presently, his frame quivered, his eyes opened, and he turned to look at me. But as I looked into his eyes an indefinable fear possessed me. The horse stared dumbly for a moment, and his nostrils dilated. Although I half-expected him to tear his head out of the halter and prance round upon me, I could not move. I stared, and as I stared, the horse's lips moved back from the teeth in a grin unmistakably a grin, of malign intelligence. The gesture vividly recalled Dearth to my mind. I had described him as equine, and if proof of the word's aptness were needed, Dandy had supplied that proof.

"He's come back," Monica murmured to me, on my return to the house. "Ill, I think. He's gone to lie down. Have you seen Dandy?"

"Yes. And I hope not to see him again."

But I was to see him again, twice again. The first time was that same night, from my bedroom window. Both my bedroom and my cousin's looked out upon that grassy hill of which I spoke. It rose for a few yards until almost level with the second story of the house and then abruptly curved away. Somewhere about midnight, feeling restless and troubled by my thoughts, I got out of bed and went to the window to take an airing.

I was not the only restless creature that night. Standing not twenty yards away, with the sky for background, was a great horse. The moon-

light made its white flank gleam like silver, and
lit up the eyes that stared fixedly at my window.

III

For sixteen days and nights we lived, Monica
and I, in the presence of this fear, a fear none
the less real for being non-susceptible of defini-
tion. The climax came suddenly, without any
sort of warning, unless Dearth's idiotic hostility
towards myself could be regarded as a warning.
The utterly unfounded idea that I was making
love to his wife had taken root in the man's
mind, and every day his manner to me became
more openly vindictive. This was the cue for
my departure, with warm thanks for my delightful holiday; but I didn't choose to take it. I
wasn't exactly in love with Monica, but she was
my comrade in danger and I was reluctant to
leave her to face her nightmare terrors alone.

The most cheerful room in that house was
the kitchen, with its red-tiled floor, its oak
rafters, and its great open fire-place. And when
in the evenings the lamp was lit and we sat there,
listening in comfort to the everlasting gale that
raged round the house, I could almost have
imagined myself happy, had it not been for the
presence of my reluctant host. He was a skeleton
at a feast, if you like! By God, we were a genial
party. From seven o'clock to ten we would sit
there, the three of us, fencing off silence with the
most pitiful of small talk. On this particular

night I had been chaffing him gently, though
with intention, about his fancy for keeping a
loaded rifle hanging over the kitchen mantelpiece ; but at last I sickened of the pastime, and
the conversation, which had been sustained only
by my efforts, lapsed. I stared at the red
embers in the grate, stealing a glance now and
again at Monica to see how she was enduring
the discomfort of such a silence. The cheap
alarum clock ticked loudly, in the way that cheap
alarum clocks have. When I looked again at
Dearth he appeared to have fallen asleep. I say
" appeared," for I instantly suspected him of
shamming sleep in order to catch us out. I knew
that he believed us to be in love with each other,
and his total lack of evidence must have occasioned him hours of useless fury. I suspected
him of the most melodramatic intentions : of
hoping to see a caress pass between us that would
justify him in making a scene. In that scene, as I
figured it, the gun over the mantelpiece might
play an important part. I don't like loaded guns.

The sight of his closed lids exasperated me
into a bitter speech designed for him to over-
hear. " Monica, your husband is asleep. He
is asleep only in order that he may wake at the
chosen moment and pour out the contents of
his vulgar little mind upon our heads."

This tirade astonished her, as well it might.
She glanced up, first at me, then at her husband ;
and upon him her eyes remained fixed. " He's not
asleep," she said, rising slowly out of her chair,

" I know he's not," I replied.

By now she was at his side, bending over him. " No," she remarked coolly. " He's dead."

At those words the wind outside redoubled its fury, and it seemed as though all the anguish of the world was in its wail. The spirit of Dearth's Farm was crying aloud in a frenzy that shook the house, making all the windows rattle. I shuddered to my feet. And in the moment of my rising the wail died away, and in the lull I heard outside the window a sudden sound of feet, of pawing, horse's feet. My horror found vent in a sort of desperate mirth.

" No, not dead. James Dearth doesn't die so easily."

Shocked by my levity, she pointed mutely to the body in the chair. But a wild idea possessed me, and I knew that my wild idea was the truth. " Yes," I said, " that may be dead as mutton. But James Dearth is outside, come to spy on you and me. Can't you hear him ? "

I stretched out my hand to the blind cord. The blind ran up with a rattle, and, pressed against the window, looking in upon us, was the face of the white horse, its teeth bared in a malevolent grin. Without losing sight of the thing for a moment, I backed towards the fire. Monica, divining my intention, took down the gun from its hook and yielded it to my desirous fingers. I took deliberate aim, and shot.

And then, with the crisis over, as I thought,

my nerves went to rags. I sat down limply, Monica huddled at my feet; and I knew with a hideous certitude that the soul of James Dearth, violently expelled from the corpse that lay outside the window, was in the room with me, seeking to re-enter that human body in the chair. There was a long moment of agony during which I trembled on the verge of madness, and then a flush came back into the dead pallid cheeks, the body breathed, the eyes opened. . . . I had just enough strength left to drag myself out of my seat. I saw Monica's eyes raised to mine; I can never for a moment stop seeing them. Three hours later I stumbled into the arms of the station-master, who put me in the London train under the impression that I was drunk. Yes, I left alone. I told you I wasn't a courageous man. . . .

IV

Bailey's voice abruptly ceased. The tension in my listening mind snapped, and I came back with a jerk, as though released by a spring, to my seat in the teashop. Bailey's queer eyes glittered across at me for a moment, and then, their light dying suddenly out, they became infinitely weary of me and of all the sorry business of living. A rationalist in grain, I find it impossible to accept the story quite as it stands. Substantially true it may be, probably is, but that it has been distorted by the prism of Bailey's singular personality I can hardly doubt. But the angle of that distortion must remain a matter for conjecture.

No such dull reflections came then to mar my appreciation of the quality of the strange hush that followed his last words. Neither of us spoke. An agitated waitress made us aware that the shop was closing, and we went into the street without a word. The rain was unremitting. I shrank back into the shelter of the porch while I fastened the collar of my mackintosh, and when I stepped out upon the pavement again, Bailey had vanished into the darkness.

I have never ceased to be vexed at losing him, and never ceased to fear that he may have thought the loss not unwelcome to me. My only hope is that he may read this and get into touch with me again, so that I may discharge my debt to him. It is a debt that lies heavily on my conscience—the price of this story, less one pound.

From " The Street of the Eye"

SLEEPING BEAUTY

HARRIET leaned across the scullery sink, where dirty plates were soaking, in order to get a better view of the moon. Her sleeves were turned up to the elbow. Her right hand grasped a ball of dishcloth from which slimy water oozed between her red fingers to float, in black spots, upon the surface of the water. Upon that water, through which projected a tureen, like the bows of a wrecked ship, the moonlight fell. The three-and-elevenpenny alarum clock in the kitchen began striking nine.

All Harriet's spiritual crises had had this scullery for their setting, or so it now seemed to Harriet herself. Seven years earlier she had stood where she was now standing and had wrestled with overmastering fear, to the accompaniment of that same ticking clock and to the drip-drip from the plate-rack upon already washed spoons. She had leaned then across the sink, as she was leaning now, and stared in terror at an unearthly glow in the sky that could scarcely fail to mean the end of the world and the coming of God in judgment. She shuddered to picture the dead bodies, putty-coloured, rising in their shrouds to confront—with her and Mamma and Alice and Maud—an implacable Creator. " O

God, don't come yet!" It had been the most spontaneous of all her prayers. She had heard too much of this God to trust herself readily to His mercy; and she, the most wicked of girls, had little enough to hope from mere justice. She had too often deceived her teacher and been unsympathetic with her poor mother; and far too often had she resented having to drudge in the house—sweep and dust, make beds, empty slops, and wash dirty dinner-things —while still at school, and to the neglect of her home-lessons.

Whether in answer to her prayer, or from some other cause, God had stayed His coming on that occasion, and to-night, within a week of her twentieth birthday, she was thinking of quite other things: not of God, but of the moon. There was something placid and sisterly to-night about that celestial presence, and Harriet was deliciously aware of a bond between them. "Because Geoff likes us both," she said in her heart. What had been his phrase, the phrase that had astonished her first to gladness? "Gentle as moonlight, soft and gentle as moonlight." The words haunted her memory like singing birds. Geoff's liking was in itself strange enough: the degree of his liking was scarcely credible. Why had he no eyes for Alice, the acknowledged beauty of the family?—or for Maud, with her brains? "Cinderella and the Ugly Sisters," Geoff had said. But Cinderella had been a pretty girl, and she, Harriet, was all too plain. It could only have been kindness or perverse obstinacy that had made him deny that. She glanced into the tiny mirror that hung from a nail on the pink-distempered wall, and examined with some distaste the oval olive face, the fair hair, and the large brown eyes that looked out at her. Tears began to form in those eyes. " Now don't start that silliness ! " she admonished herself. And she returned to the practical world and to the washing of the things dirtied at supper. " I do wish Mamma wouldn't leave all her fat," she thought, as with her scullery knife she sped three quivering fragments into the waste-pail.

There remained the undeniable fact that Geoff wanted to marry her : that is, he liked her so much that he wished her to share his home, when he acquired one, and wash his dishes instead of her mother's. She could cook, too : she could make him nice things ; and she would indeed have cheerfully slaved for his comfort in gratitude for that pity which, as she supposed, had made his glance linger in kindness upon her. But that was not to be. Even in that wonderful moment when he praised her gentleness she had realized how impossible it was that she should leave Mamma ; and her sisters had been not slow to emphasize that impossibility. " Boy and girl flirtation," said Alice with genial contempt : unaccountably, since Geoff was twenty-six and considered to be rather a clever young man. He was a poet—

a bank-clerk in his spare time—and his knack of finding rhymes should alone have earned him some respect. To Geoff himself Alice had always been conspicuously friendly; and as for Maud —he had been her friend in the first place (she had met him in the City), and it had always been assumed that it was Maud whom he came to see. But about Geoff's intentions now there could be no doubt at all. He had even wanted, the dear silly, to help Harriet wash up, but she had not dared to allow that, and he, making a virtue of necessity, was at this moment closeted with the family, perhaps urging once more his extravagant claim.

The last dish dried, the last fork placed in its proper section of the plate-basket, she returned, rather shamefaced, to the sitting-room. As the door closed behind her an ominous hush fell. A smile upon the proud plump face of Alice froze hard and thawed suddenly. Maud swung round upon the revolving music-stool and began turning the pages of Mendelssohn's *Lieder*. Her mother, perched insecurely on the edge of her chair, visibly suffered. She was always visibly suffering.

"Girls!" said Mamma plaintively. . . . It was enough. Harriet's sisters rose without a word and left the room. Mamma looked at the young man, but he made no movement. "Geoffrey!" she said, a world of pathos in her voice. But Geoffrey was deaf to it. "This concerns me, too," he said. "May I smoke?"

"Very well. Stay, if you wish to be cruel . . ."
But this man, lost to all sense of humanity, only
replied : "I'm vulgarly persistent, no doubt,
but you see I happen to want Harry."

Harry's mother turned twin orbs of suffering
upon her daughter, and began reciting the
speech she had prepared.

"I'm sorry, Harriet, to disappoint you. I
understand your desire to get away from a
troublesome invalid mother and your two
bread-winning sisters. But you are God's
charge to me and I must protect you."

"From me?" inquired Geoffrey.

She did not heed the interruption.

"I say nothing against Geoffrey, but I can't
consent to anything in the shape of an engagement between you. For one thing you are as
yet a mere girl ; you know nothing of life and
nothing of marriage. And that isn't all. Geoffrey
has told me something very sad. He has been
very open and frank with me : I *will* say that for
him. We all like Geoffrey. But he's told me
that he would wish to be married in an office.
He has queer views, my dear. He even tells me
that he only goes to church to please his mother
and father. I'm afraid he's let go of the Saviour's
hand altogether. After that I need hardly say
more. I know my little Harriet too well to
believe that she can wish to give mother pain.
I already have my Cross to bear."

"Very well, Mamma." Harriet's eyes were
luminous with tears.

At that Geoffrey rose. "Then I'd better clear off home at once."

"My dear Geoffrey," protested his hostess, "I know you are thinking to spare my feelings after this upset. You're very good to me always. But you'll please stay your week-end. We mustn't part in unfriendliness—and you know how I should hate you to travel on Sunday."

He could not keep bitterness out of his smile, but he replied cheerfully enough :

"Well, Mrs Mason, since Harry is not to be engaged to me there'll be no harm in my taking her out for half an hour before bed ? Would you care to come, Harry ? . . . Thanks awfully."

II

Harriet went to her room in a trembling ecstasy, struggling against odds to believe that she was indeed beautiful, as he had said. While she moved about, within the pink beflowered walls of her very own room (as in her heart she was wont to call it), his voice still made music in her memory.

"Why will you submit to be boxed up in that prison ? Can't you understand how I want you ? Can't you understand how lovely you are ? " He had never before been so passionate in his iterations. And she could only shake her head, elated, yet with secret misgiving. He had very queer ideas, Mamma had said. Was this obsession by the thought of beauty perhaps one of them ? But there was worse to follow.

"Harry, are you determined to give me up ?"

She replied miserably: "I can't go against Mamma. You wouldn't have me go against Mamma. Oh, Geoff, I would do anything else for you."

The words were like a match dropped in dry stubble. "Then you do love me ? You do ! You do ! "

His violence frightened and braced her. "You know I like you tremendously," she said, grappling with the unknown, "better than anyone else in the world."

"Except your mother," he retorted bitterly, and then added in a changed tone : "Harry darling, we've never kissed. Do you like me enough for that ? We may never have another moment alone."

"Of course, you funny boy ! "

He bent towards her, and she kissed him, in friendly fashion, on the cheek. "Happy now ? " she asked, almost merrily, hoping to drive away his tragic air.

He smiled. "Not exactly." An odd smile it was. And at the bend of the road, under the shadow of Mrs Lavender's lime trees, he took her face suddenly between his hands and kissed her mouth. Something stirred in her, but did not awake. She could not understand his emotion.

160

" Harry, you said you'd do anything for me. Did you mean it ? "

" Yes."

" You'll think me strange. Perhaps you'll be shocked. It's this : let me see you. If I'm to go away from you, as I must, let me see you just once, as you really are. Give me a memory to take with me."

Was he indeed mad ? Poor Geoff ! " But, dear, you can see me now."

" Your face, your clothes. Let me see *you*, all your beauty. . . ."

She burned with shame as something of his meaning dawned on her . . . and now, as she stood in her bedroom re-living the scene, the plan he had unfolded seemed both wild and wicked. Wild and wicked, yes : yet shot through with a flash of poetry. An illuminated " Thou God seest me " gleamed at her from one wall, and a pledge to abstain by God's help from all intoxicating liquors as beverages, signed in childish calligraphy *Harriet Mason*, accused her from another. Wild and wicked ; but in a passion of gratitude for being loved, and for the spark kindled within her, she had yielded her promise.

" Thou God seest me." Blushing hotly, very conscious of that inquisitive eye, she took down her hair. With a miniature clatter the pins fell from nerveless fingers on to the glass surface of the dressing-table. Slowly she undressed ; paused a moment, shyly stroking her slim nude body; and then with a gesture of resolve, slipped into her kimono. The eye of God was still upon her, but she had given her word.

Her woolly slippers made no sound on the oilcloth floor. She opened her door and stepped into the passage. Opposite her was Geoff's door, left purposely ajar. Tremblingly, but swiftly lest fear should make her false, she crossed and entered. Geoff made no sound. She stood, too ashamed to look up, pushing his door to with a nervous backward movement of the hand. It closed, not without noise.

Her lips moved, as in prayer. She lifted her arms high, and her garment, slipping from white shoulders, fell and clustered at her feet, a diaphanous shimmering mass.

"Lovely, lovely . . . O God!" The scarce-heard whisper made her heart leap in exultation. She raised her head and looked steadfastly at her love. He sat up in bed, still as an image of adoration, the moonlight making visible the worship in his eyes. She stooped, gathered up her gown, and went out into the passage . . . into the arms of Alice.

"I heard a door slam," said Alice. "What's the matter? Why, you've—— That's Geoff's room!"

Alice became pale and for a moment speechless with anger. When she recovered her tongue it was to use a language strange to the ears of Harriet.

"I don't know what you mean," cried Harriet,

starry-eyed, " and I don't care. He loves me, Alice, because I am so beautiful, beautiful. Why didn't you tell me I was beautiful ? "

She pushed past Alice and locked herself in her bedroom. Those bitter reproaches had no sting for her. Even had she understood them they would have been less than a feather's weight against the joy now born in her heart. For her the world was made new, clean and new. With beauty, seen hitherto through a glass darkly, she was now face to face. She fell asleep exhausted with happiness, and when in the morning Mamma came to her room and sobbed, and raved, she could understand not a word of it.

" You've brought disgrace and shame upon us all, you wretched child ! " And to this Harriet, in her profound innocence, could only answer : " But we love each other, Mamma. What harm have we done ? "

" You shall leave my house as soon as that man can be made to marry you, and never come back again."

" Am I to marry Geoff after all, then, Mamma ? "

Yes, it appeared that she was, and that her daring to ask the question was further proof of her shamelessness. It was all very baffling.

From " The Street of the Eye "

163

SIMPSON'S FUNERAL

THEY came from the four points of the compass to Simpson's funeral; yet when all the guests were assembled they numbered no more than fifteen. A scattered family, but a faithful one nevertheless. They had spread a fine network of correspondence, like a spider's web, all over England. The hundred small jealousies, the rankling memories, and the necessity for taking sides in the great subterranean quarrel between Simpson and his wife: these had seldom or never been allowed to ripple the surface of that correspondence, still less to stop it. Whatever happened, little George's operation for rupture must be reported to his grandfather; however derelict from his own duties, Lucy's uncle must be invited to share the general disapprobation of Lucy's engagement to a penniless Channel Islander of unknown antecedents. As grandfather, as uncle, Simpson had been an unqualified success. "Very likely," his daughters would say. "You don't have to live with him, my dears."

The house was in a state of quiet, mournful, important bustle. Aunt Elizabeth, clutching a little wad of pocket-handkerchief, tiptoed into the room where lilies shed their ghastly pallor and their sickly perfume. She stepped with an exaggerated care, closing the door softly, as if in fear of waking her dead brother. A mean little room with a florid wall-paper and crowded with heavy furniture : an old walnut piano, a mahogany table pushed into a corner to make room for the coffin, a bookcase full of unread Victorian classics, a sofa shrouded in a dust-sheet. A large gilt ormolu clock stood on the mantel-piece, flanked by family photographs and lustre-ware. Curtains draped the French windows, and a thick gloom, compounded of scent and dusk and summer heat, pervaded the room like a personal presence. Everything here was mere lumber now, including Simpson himself. Eliza-beth recoiled from the thought even in the moment of entertaining it. The dim atmosphere pressed cold fingers upon her mind ; the slow ticking of the clock—a clock he had always hated —tapped into her heart a message of complete indifference. While she stood, looking and listening, that ticking came to an abrupt end, leaving the room in the possession of a silence that was more than Elizabeth could endure. In that moment of paralysis, that nightmare of atrophied volition, she stood in an eternal tomb, all existence seeming to her tortured fancy no more than a tale of deaths. First one, then another ; and no knowing on whom next the doom would fall. First her child, then her husband, and now her favourite brother. Shivering, as with mortal cold, she turned back to the door. "Everything in perfect taste," said her lips dutifully; and they repeated the phrase to her niece, Edith Simpson, who awaited her in the corridor. "Such nice flowers, my dear," added Aunt Elizabeth, bravely resuming her necessary *rôle*.

Edith nodded, and kissed the older woman's cheek. With a little encouragement she would have burst into tears once again. She was preoccupied with grief, and felt it right that she should be so preoccupied. Somewhere at the back of her mind was the conviction that never for one moment must she forget that her father was dead, her mother broken-hearted, and herself left burdened with sorrow and untold responsibility. It troubled her secretly that thoughts of this and that would sometimes intrude to seduce her from this undeviating fidelity. There were so many things to be done, arrangements to be made, people to be written to, condolences to be acknowledged; but she herself had held aloof from these tedious distractions. They would have provided a relief of sorts, forgetfulness; and that was the last thing she desired. All her mind and soul must be concentrated upon the dark task of mourning: that was her debt, and she would pay it in full. Anything else, anything more active, would have been less than right and proper. Luckily there was Rose, her youngest and only married sister, to help see after things. On Rose Burnett's young shoulders rested the conduct of nearly all these merely practical affairs. She had come, in response to a telegram, bringing with her (since he could not be left at home untended) her three-year-old son; and, promptly upon her appearance, Mrs Simpson had retired to nurse her grief and her grievance in sensational solitude, and Edith had given herself up to the feeding of that emotion with periodic visits. Thankful as she was for Rose's capable domestic management, she could not stifle the reproachful feeling that there was something a little callous in such efficiency. But Rose, of course, having a husband and a child, could not be expected to cower under the blow as did those to whom poor Father had been everything, everything. Extraordinary, nevertheless, how selfish marriage had made her.

Edith loved Aunt Elizabeth because Aunt Elizabeth was a member of the family, her father's sister; and family sentiment so far triumphed over the natural antipathy that divided the two women as to impel them, for a brief moment, into each other's arms. Edith kissed her aunt with mournful emphasis, receiving in return a peck and a pat on the shoulder that were altogether too brisk, she thought, for such an occasion. Elizabeth was, in fact, a little disconcerted by the embrace, which she divined to be more ritualistic than affectionate. She disengaged herself, murmuring "Cheer up, my dear," and walked unsteadily down the corridor that led to the room where the other guests were collected. She overtook Rose.

"Where's Master Dickie?" she asked, with an attempt at mild gaiety.

"In the garden, I think," Rose answered, "talking to Uncle Harry. . . . Has everybody arrived?"

"All except Uncle Tom. It isn't like him to be late. What can have happened?"

Rose shrugged her shoulders, which was the nearest she ever permitted herself to a shudder. "Oh, don't talk about things happening! He was written to, right enough." Rose wrinkled her brow, giving, in that moment, a hint of what she would look like at thirty-five. Small, brown, comely, she seemed to Elizabeth a gallant, pathetic figure, prematurely burdened with the responsibilities of middle-age. "Written to, and telephoned. Telephoned at once."

"Of course," nodded Aunt Elizabeth. "He's the executor, I suppose. Being unpunctual is one of his professional tricks, no doubt." She spoke good-humouredly, as if bantering the absent brother.

They joined the rest of the family, who were in the morning-room, pulling on new black gloves, staring gloomily out of the window, or fidgeting with this or that part of their attire. All were self-conscious and miserable, wishing the hateful business over. The only man among them who seemed to be, even for a moment, unaware of his surroundings was Edward Simpson, the youngest of the dead man's brothers. He was absorbed in his own thoughts, from which no parade of horror seemed able to distract him. He was wishing he had kept in closer touch with poor old Fred. There had never been anything but good feeling between the two, but they had drifted apart, circumstances aiding, and Edward had been at no pains to arrest the drift. For that he now blamed himself bitterly. Fred had not prospered, either in love or in business, as he, Edward, had prospered. His marriage had not been an unqualified success, nor had it been that next-best thing, a complete and recognized failure. So much Edward surmised, and had surmised long ago. Sitting now, in the house of mourning, tapping with his fingers on the arms of his chair and absently scrutinizing his boots, pictures of the past pressed upon him, bringing with them stabbing intimations of a sympathy, a brotherly bond, that might have been and now could never be. Sometimes, once or twice a year, perhaps, the two men had met in the City, where business took them both every weekday of their lives, and lunched together, exchanging polite gossip. Edward remembered vividly the last of such occasions, remembered, with a fresh and poignant emotion, how old, how *tired*, his brother had looked. The grey-white hair and the lined features were those of a man prematurely aged at sixty, but the eyes, though infinitely weary, held still a hint of the pathetic eagerness of youth. They were the eyes of a boy, eyes sick with disappointment, yet still timid, in fugitive

6*

moments, with a kind of hurt surprise, a wistfulness. Well, he would never look like that again. Whatever his troubles had been, they were over now. . . . But the trite reflection did but add fuel to the fire of Edward's brooding contrition. Suddenly he was overwhelmed by an invasion of earlier, more cruel memories: he was once more the little brother, and Fred, magnificent from boarding-school, was giving him the cigarette-pictures he had deigned to collect during the term for him. Edward's hands leaped to his face to shut him in with his memories. Then he became aware that he was in a roomful of people, and he stiffened. "Uncle Tom not come yet, Rose?" he inquired briskly.

They all, the women in particular, felt some compunction about setting off without Tom, the dead man's eldest brother. Even Elizabeth, his senior by six years, felt that she hardly dared acquiesce in the disposal of these mortal remains until the masterful head of the house had admitted the sad necessity. Perhaps she nursed the foolish fancy that brother Tom, known among his acquaintances as a man not to be trifled with, could bluster even Death himself into surrender. But the funeral could not be delayed indefinitely: both for obvious reasons and because human nerves could not stand a prolongation of the ordeal, the decisive step must be taken. Everything was ready. The mourners filed into the dingy hall, and down the gravel path; with ill-concealed eagerness to be done with it all they scrambled into the waiting carriages. Rose remained behind, tearless and stricken, to minister to the frankly helpless Edith. A brace of young aunts and a female cousin by marriage sighed and sniffed in the background. And still the newly made widow dominated the scene by her absence. And still Uncle Tom did not come.

II

He came, however, at four o'clock, when the others returned. He volunteered no explanation of his conduct, and no one had the courage to demand it of him. He looked to be, and was, a hale, elderly, and astute London solicitor. He dominated his brothers and sisters by the sheer force of his insensitiveness, his difference from themselves. Instinctively they turned to him, as to something solid, rather stupid, but thoroughly reliable. He offered, with his loud-voiced, matter-of-fact air, and his preoccupation with business matters, an asylum from sentiment. Among this older generation of Simpsons he alone had never dallied, however idly, with thoughts of art. Edward, compromising between ambition and necessity, had made himself a first-class poster-designer. Harry had secretly circulated among his friends a volume of pastoral poems. Frederick, having lost his way and strayed into the employ of a commercial firm, had hankered all his life to practise architecture.

Even Elizabeth had a pretty talent for water-colour painting. But Tom, proud though he was of his mother's other children, was supremely content to be unlike them. He knew himself to be a highly successful professional man, and he was grimly happy in the knowledge. While others trifled with playthings of the mind, exploiting their own unimportant emotions, he shouldered the work of the world.

It was to execute a duty that he was here now, and for no idle purpose. Sincerely as he regretted his brother's death, there was a touch of exasperation in his regret. It was so like poor Fred, always a bit of a bungler, to get ill and die at the ridiculously early age of sixty-one. Tom's bearing, as they all took their seats at the tea-table, suggested not so much that a man's life had ended as that a business had gone irreparably wrong, and that he, Tom, presiding over a creditors' meeting, was determined to make the best of a bad job.

" Yes," he admitted to his sister Elizabeth, " it was a great shock to me. Incompetent doctor, no doubt. How's Adela taking it ? "

Elizabeth shook her head. " Ah, I'm afraid she's very sadly, poor girl. And obstinate, too," added the old lady, with a nervous glance in the direction of Edith. " Yes, my dear, a wee bit stubborn. She shuts herself in her room and just gives way."

" H'm," said Tom. His disapproval needed no emphasis.

"After all," ventured Rose, timidly, "we've got to go on, haven't we?"

"You're right, my love," said Tom, with a glance of keen affection.

At this moment the door opened, and Mrs Simpson stood, a tall black figure of desolation, framed in the doorway. She paused before moving into the room. All eyes turned towards her, yet turned reluctantly, afraid to face her. All, except Edith who was too devoted, Elizabeth who was too wise, and Tom who was too complacent, felt themselves detected in a kind of disloyalty. They were conscious of having thought unkindly of her. She had shut herself away, with sorrow and mortification as her sole companions; yet they, in their secret hearts, had suspected her, at the worst of hypocrisy, at the best of self-deceiving sentimentality. Those cold eyes that had flashed so often with scorn for her husband were now bloodshot with intemperate grief for him. Those thin lips that had so often implied that his existence was a burden to her, now quivered in resentment at his having been taken from her. Yet in vain did Rose try to harden her heart against this mother; and Edward, though he could not like his sister-in-law, was not so simple as to think he understood her. Even in the moment of criticizing her tragedy-airs, her too obvious exploitation of a sentiment to which her new status entitled her, he rebuked himself with the trite reminder that

173

human emotions will not submit to tabulation. Hypocrisy there might be ; but might there not be genuine grief as well ? And who could say which was the more fundamental ? Harry did not bother with such problems ; the miscellany of junior aunts, uncles, and cousins savoured the drama of Adela's entry without analysing it ; and Tom was unaware that any problem existed. He had summed up his brother's wife years before, and had placed her definitely in a category in his mind from which she would never escape. "The woman's acting ! " he said to himself ; and was content to leave it at that.

If Adela Simpson was acting, Edith lost no time in responding to her cue. She pushed her untouched plate away, and ran to her mother's side, grasped her hand with tender solicitude, and murmured inaudibly. A storm of weeping seemed imminent, but Tom was in no mood to tolerate such a discomfort.

He came forward with hand outstretched.

"Well, Adela, how are you ? Come along and have some of your own tea. I wanted to wait for you, but Edith insisted that we shouldn't. Regular martinet, your daughter, eh ? "

He took masterful possession of Mrs Simpson, and led her to the table.

"And after tea," added Uncle Tom, "a few of us will get together and talk business."

Mrs Simpson made one futile attempt to resist this domination. "My fatherless girls . . ." she began.

"Are adequately provided for," said Uncle Tom. "The brown bread and butter, if you please, Rose! . . . Thank you, my dear."

III

And after tea, obedient to a hint, all the juniors and cousins and relations-in-law left the house, leaving the leaders of the clan to talk business. Rose, at her own request, was absent from the conference; but she could not escape its consequences. She greeted her mother, an hour later, when that afflicted lady suffered herself to be led by Edith from the presence of the informative Tom. But Rose's greeting went unanswered, perhaps unnoticed. In her mother's eyes she read a familiar story. The anger that Simpson's death had magically transmuted into self-pity now flamed again in his widow's mien.

"Mother!" Rose cried. "What is the matter?" She turned in her distress and bewilderment to Edith. "What is it, Edith? What has happened?"

Edith, with a dumb gesture of helplessness, passed on. Rose repeated her question to Aunt Elizabeth.

"My dear," said Aunt Elizabeth, "it's time I went back home. Walk a little way to the station with me."

"But what has made Mother look so dreadful?"

175

"Nothing to worry about. . . . Wait while I get my things on."

On the way to the station Rose learned the little that the old lady could tell her.

"Your mother said such hard, cruel things, my dear. I'm not sure I can forgive her. But I ought not to have gone without saying good-bye. No, that was wrong of me. It was, indeed."

Simpson had left a hundred pounds out of his meagre estate to an unknown woman : that was the salient fact that emerged from Aunt Elizabeth's confused account. "And your mother, my dear, puts the very worst con-struction on it. Your Uncle Tom did his best to hide it. But she would know everything. And now she knows she doesn't like it."

"But," cried Rose, "is Mother left unpro-vided for ? "

"Your mother has a pension from the firm, of course. And there's plenty besides. It's not the money. It's . . . it's . . . oh, you're not such a child as not to understand."

"Yes, I understand," confessed Rose. She understood : perhaps better than anyone she understood. But, somehow, she was unable to feel humiliated, indignant, at the possibility of her father's secret life. She was excited by the romantic suggestions of this dramatic disclosure ; she at once pitied her father, and envied him. And, above all, she was glad, defiantly glad, that there had been at least one

176

flash of passionate poetry in his dull and thwarted existence. She could not imagine him as anything but the old man he had been for some ten years or more. Earlier memories were blurred. She saw him now as she had last seen him: a thin, emaciated old man, with a white stubbly beard beginning to grow in flesh that seemed frail as tissue-paper. She saw his hands beating a tremulous tattoo on the sheets of his bed; she heard his gallant attempt at gaiety in response to her greeting. Such a kindly, helpless old man; and so utterly at the mercy of the pain that racked him.

The broken voice of Aunt Elizabeth broke in upon her musing. "Don't think ill of your dear father," said Aunt Elizabeth. The next moment, "Oh, Rose," she cried, with trembling lip, " he was such a pretty baby ! "

From " The Baker's Cart "

THE PURITAN

Nᴏᴛ until they reached the hotel, to be confronted by a hard-faced image in black,
did the poor fellow realize some of the more
odious possibilities of their situation. " Will you
register, please," said the image, discovering to
the eyes of the shy couple a mouthful of yellow
fangs. Another barbarous survival from war-
time, he thought ; and he did his best not to
behave like a suspected person. He grasped the
proffered pen with an eagerness that he knew,
the moment after, to have been over-acted.
With a bold flourish he wrote *T. F. Heywood* in
the register. When he had handed the pen to
Pauline, an idiotic mistrust of her memory set
him watching her hand, furtively, as it scratched,
with spluttering emphasis, the unaccustomed
surname. But no, she had it pat. She had
written it often enough, indeed, to have it pat.
But only on envelopes : a signature was another
matter. However, she produced, he was quick
to observe, a very tolerable signature, having
just that touch of character which gives to a
signature the air of authenticity. Heywood—
though he would never have admitted it—
was just a little shocked by her cleverness. It
was almost cynical of her to take things so easily.

178

But perhaps a little cynicism was only to be expected in a woman so thoroughly married and so unhappily. By "thoroughly," Heywood meant "legally," but he meant much more than that : he meant, to be specific, the two children whose existence he was trying, with a kind of angry determination, to forget. And he meant the ten years during which Pauline had been, in fact, as she was still in name, the wife of another man. Ten years was such a deuce of a long time. Heywood believed, as he worried the thought of that decade in his dog-and-bone fashion, that had it been only eight years, or even nine, he would have felt happier. There was something solid about ten years of intimacy, a kind of confident rotundity that could not be wished away. As Pauline preceded him into the lift that was to take them to the fourth floor, he glanced at the back of her head and was angered by her serene bearing. It was as if, having been unfaithful to him for ten years, she was now coolly taking his love and his forgiveness for granted. And yet, he reflected, with melancholy satisfaction, she might well be sure of herself and of him. He had always loved her, and she knew it. He had loved her and wooed her before her marriage ; he had loved her, tragically and at a respectful distance, during her marriage ; and who else should have been chosen to rescue her from a loveless home, a monotonous domestic routine ? Who, indeed ! Nothing in the world could win him from his loyalty. That, surely, he was proving at this moment.

Arrived at the fourth floor, they were conducted by the lift attendant to their room, Number 480. Mustn't forget that number. The lift attendant glanced at Pauline in a way that convinced Heywood, for one insane second, that the fellow knew her to be Mrs George Duthoit. But the moment the door had closed on them that thought vanished. Heywood and Pauline faced each other across the width of the bedroom. Although he averted his eyes from it, Heywood was acutely conscious of the bed, as though it had been a third person. He smothered an impulse to bow himself out of the room with a conventional apology for his intrusion, and met Pauline's glance bravely. She said nothing for a moment, and he read embarrassment into her silence. It comforted him profoundly and set him glowing with chivalrous sentiment : he felt that he could contrive to forget his own misgiving in the act of dispelling hers.

"Oh, Tom," she said at length.

"My dear girl, what is it ? "

"The fourth floor. What bad luck ! "

"Why is it bad luck ? "

"Suppose there should be a fire in the night ! "

Good God !—in a delicate situation like this was that all the woman thought about ! Here was Heywood making ready to argue away her doubts and fears about the . . . well, the propriety of the step they were taking together, and all she worried about was the possibility of being burned to death in the night. So disconcerted was he that he quite forgot to say, as he would have done in less compromising circumstances, " I will save you, darling—or, at the worst, we will die together." And then, with an abrupt change of mood, he cursed himself for his obtuseness. This fear of fire was, of course, no more than tactful affectation, designed to dissipate the embarrassment of the moment. Tenderness flooded his heart once more. His eyes gloated protectively over her.

" You're not unhappy, Pauline ? You don't regret anything ? "

She replied, with a little laugh, " What makes you ask that ? "

He glided to her side, took her hand, pressed it fervently. " You know, you do know, don't you, Pauline, that there's nothing wrong in . . . what we're doing ? "

" Wrong ? " echoed Pauline. Like a puzzled child. It was as if she had never heard the word before. There was no mistaking her attitude this time. This was not tact : it was sheer ingenuous innocence, and to poor Heywood it seemed, in the circumstances, the very height of indelicacy. Had the dear girl no conscience at all ? Was it possible that she had not been properly brought up ? He persisted in his quest for some sign of grace in her, some sign of shame.

" I'm anxious," he murmured, having touched

her brow with his lips, " that you shouldn't have the least little twinge of misgiving. I want you to understand that he has no real claim on you at all, since there is no love between you. Ours is the true marriage : that other was only counterfeit. Whatever the world may think " —but he couldn't help wincing when he remembered what the world would think—" you are more truly respectable in your new life than you were in the old. There's nothing to be ashamed of . . ."

Pauline stared at Heywood as though he had indeed been, as a moment before he had felt himself to be, an intrusive stranger. But she spoke gently.

" You funny darling ! I never supposed there was. Why this sudden orgy of self-justification ? "

" Then that's all right," he said, a little stiff in manner, as who would not be with a woman who missed all her cues ? " You're very fortunate to be able to take life so serenely."

" Is there another way of taking it ? I didn't know," she remarked coolly, but not, he could swear, quite without malice. " Tell me, Tommy, is your little conscience bothering you ? "

Heywood felt that the moral gulf between them was widening. She spoke of conscience as though it were a kind of toothache ; in another moment she would perhaps be offering him aspirin for it. His tenderness for her was melting away. No man, not even a devoted lover, cares to have his moments of high serious-

182

ness dismissed, however kindly, as symptoms of hypochondria.

" In the circumstances, no ! " he replied firmly, and tried to believe what he said. " I feel that your husband, I mean your late husband, has put himself out of court, so to speak, by his treatment of you. For one thing, I have very good reason to believe that he has formed another attachment. I only hope it hasn't gone too far."

" Too far ? Why ? "

Heywood coughed, and turned his glance towards the window, which looked out on a prospect of chimney-pots and grey brick wall. " If he has been unfaithful to you," he said, addressing his remarks to a trinity of plump red chimney-pots, " there may be difficulty about the divorce." He turned to her with an impulsive gesture. " Oh, darling, won't it be good when it's all over, and you and I can get married and settle down ! "

" Won't it be nice," she responded, as he put his arm round her shoulder, " so nice and legal." He withdrew his arm hastily, as though she had repulsed him. She noticed the abruptness of the action, and glanced at him mischievously. " Isn't that what you meant, Tommy ? I'm sorry. I thought it was."

The shadow on his face did not lift. Things were going all awry. He had not bargained for this. It came to his mind, with a stab of surprise, that never before, in all their ten years' friendship, had he exchanged intimate opinions with Pauline. For long enough they had talked only of books and pictures and music, tennis and motoring, with occasional footnotes on stock-broking. And latterly their conversation had revolved round the inexhaustible theme of Pauline's unhappiness and Heywood's determination to remove it. On all his pictures of the future they were to share together there was the high gloss of his sentimental philosophy. They constituted a series of well-polished oleographs. His life with Pauline was to be a long and beautiful romance, full of chaste ecstasy, and oh, so spiritual! He had not lost hope of finding some broadminded cleric who would consent to bestow on their marriage the blessing of Holy Church.

" Cheer up," said Pauline, remorseful for her felinity. " Tommy lad, Tommy lad, you're a funny little chap." This was one of her favourite ways of bantering him into happiness. It seldom failed to make him grin, but it failed now. Pauline continued her song : " But you're long and you're strong. Soon you'll scorn your father's lap."

No visible effect. Piqued by her failure, she added, with an abrupt return to her former mood : " Well, not soon. But some day, perhaps. . . . If you'd prefer to withdraw from this engagement of ours, Tommy, it's not too late, you know."

He turned upon her almost angrily. " Of

course it's too late. . . . Besides," he added,
" I don't want to withdraw. You know I don't.
I love you. I want to make you my wife. More
than ever I love you."

" You make it sound like a piece of Coué
drill," said Pauline. " Every day and in every
way . . ." She saw the pain in his face, and
ran to him, full of contrition, with arms outstretched. " Forgive me, darling. I'm a dreadful tease."

Ah, there was the Pauline he knew and loved,
the old, warmhearted, generous Pauline ! With
a delicious sense of homecoming he gathered her
into his arms and kissed ardently her responsive
lips. And even in the midst of that spiritual
rapture there intruded a thought that made him
wince. How often had she kissed George
Duthoit in just that way ?

Released from his arms she moved across to
the dressing-table and began taking off her
jewellery. " I'm getting rather tired," she said,
" and we've got to be out early in the morning,
haven't we ? What time is the boat-train ? "

He told her the time of the boat-train. She
made no response. " Too early for you, dear ? "
he asked solicitously ; but she did not appear to
hear. She was gazing abstractedly at a photograph which she had apparently just taken from
her handbag. A little chilled, he stepped towards her.

" Oh damn ! " He smothered the exclamation
at its birth. Over Pauline's shoulder he had

caught sight of the hateful pretty faces of the little Duthoits.

Pauline turned to him radiantly. "Oh, Tommy, I forgot to show you this photo. It's a new one. It came this morning. I was on pins and needles lest it should be delayed, but it came this morning. Don't they look darlings!"

The darlings were leaning together against a photographer's gate that appeared to be on the point of collapse. "Yes," said Heywood, without enthusiasm. "Very jolly." And this was the woman to whom, not many minutes ago, he had attributed tact! Had she no conception of a man's feelings?

Not noticing his coolness, the infatuated mother pursued her theme. "Little Georgie's getting ever so knowing. He says the quaintest things. And as for Dot, although she's two years younger she's quite a little mother to him. Miss Simmons says that they're both very sharp for their ages. Some people think that precocity in children is undesirable, makes them conceited and unmanageable, but I don't agree, do you? Better than being stupid little puddings, anyhow. Don't you think so?"

"I never did care for pudding," said Heywood.

"Of course, children can be a frightful nuisance," reflected Pauline, half to herself.

"They can, indeed," agreed Heywood.

"But then I was careful not to weary myself of them. There was always their nurse at hand. Poor kids," she sighed, "I was rather impatient with them sometimes." She propped the photograph up against the dressing-table mirror, and turned away with the shadow of wistfulness in her eyes.

Heywood stared morosely at the offensive thing. For one moment he stared, and then decided to speak his mind. This could not go on.

" Pauline ! "

" Tommy ? "

" Do you propose to leave that thing there all night ? "

She was startled. " What thing ? "

He pointed, with a gesture of contempt.

" Why ? " Her face blanched. " Do you object to it ? "

" Object ? I hate it. Of course I hate it."

" State your objection," she demanded coldly, like a judge examining a prisoner.

" I will, by God," he cried, goaded beyond endurance. " Do you think I can sleep in this room to-night, in the peculiar circumstances that make to-night different from every other night ; do you think I can sleep here, I say, with that damned photograph of your children, another man's children, staring and simpering at me ? "

She smiled with exasperating patience. " Never before have I been called a peculiar circumstance. That's a new term of abuse, Tommy."

" It's not fair," burst out Heywood, his voice rising indiscreetly. " It's not fair and it's not decent. Why must I be reminded of George

187

Duthoit's children? I tell you they're indecent."

" My children—indecent? " This time she
forgot to smile.

" Yes, indecent. I repeat the word. Indecent.
They are living witnesses of your marriage to
that man. They are the sign and symbol and
incarnation of something I want to forget. To
parade your children like this—why, it's like
parading Duthoit's embraces. That's just what
they are, those children—visible embraces ! "

Pauline stared at him with a new curiosity, a
disinterested, scientific curiosity. " That's what
we all are, my dear Tommy. Did it never occur
to you before ? "

Swiftly she put on her rings again, her wristlet
watch, and finally her hat and her light summer
cloak.

" Where are you going ? "

But she was already gone. The door slammed
behind her. He dashed out into the corridor
and saw her running, positively running, towards
the stairhead. " Pauline ! Pauline ! Are you
crazy ? " She was out of sight, and he could not
pursue her and make a scene. After all, he had
no legal right . . . curse it !

Ten minutes later he was sitting disconsolately
on the bed, staring at her trunk with its label
describing her as *Mrs T. F. Heywood*. He felt
bewildered, hurt, angry, foolish ; but most of
all he felt foolish. It seemed to him inconceiv-
able that an elopement so long planned, so

eagerly awaited, could in a moment come to
nothing. For three months now this event had
been, he told himself, the only star in the sky
of his future. He cursed himself for not having
been able to conceal for a little while longer
his true feelings about those damned children.
But indeed it was not until to-day that he had
known how deep those feelings were; for not
until to-day had Pauline found it necessary to
give her maternal passion an airing. Hitherto,
at his secret meetings with her, she had been
perhaps too much occupied with himself to
spare more than a passing thought for little
Georgie and darling Dot. She had had just the
degree of mother-love necessary to true woman-
liness, and no more. Heywood conceded, being
above all things a reasonable man, that a good
woman must inevitably experience a tender
reaction towards the children she has just
abandoned; but there is such a thing as modera-
tion. He had been prepared to find her timid,
bashful, self-accusing; but he had not been
prepared for an unseemly display of affection
for his hated rivals. Still less had he reckoned
on her quick temper. Brooding bitterly, he
made pretence of congratulating himself on his
escape from a woman so shallow, so small-
minded, that she could reject the devotion of a
lifetime out of mere pique. She could never
have loved him, or she could not bear to make
him suffer so much. But this line of argument, with its distasteful conclusion, he quickly

abandoned. She loved him! There could be no doubting that she loved him! And there could be no doubting that she was, by her wilfulness, hurting herself as much as she had hurt him. Perhaps even more—ah, grateful thought! He was, as he now took occasion to remind himself, the last person in the world to wish that anybody should suffer on his account; yet he could not help feeling that if poor little Pauline was at this very moment bitterly (ah, how bitterly!) repenting her rash act, she had only herself to blame. He pictured her, huddled up in the corner of a taxi-cab, sobbing like a child, and perhaps dabbing her little nose at intervals with a wet wad of handkerchief. The picture was so vivid that he could not doubt its accuracy. After a while her convulsive movements become less frequent, for she is nearing the railway station and must compose herself in time to face the hard indifferent world. She now sits in the middle of the seat, holding herself stiffly erect, and staring straight in front of her with large despairing eyes. . . . Yes, she would suffer, and Heywood could not but feel that it was better so. He only hoped that it might all be a lesson to her; and, descending from this cloud of fantasy into the realm of fact, and confronted once more by his immediate problem of what to do next, he hoped that she would learn her lesson quickly enough to return to him before it was too late. For he was not a vindictive man. Wronged though he was, he could yet find it in his heart to forgive her. He almost smacked his lips in anticipation of the great scene which every passing minute, as he now convinced himself, brought nearer; enjoying in advance the unique luxury—the proud privilege of a strong man in dealing with a sweet woman— of taking the blame for her fault on his own broad shoulders. "Forgive me, little woman, for being such a brute." He tried that over, and it sounded very well. "Your Tommy didn't mean to be cruel." At that she would melt into his arms; her hands would cling to his shoulders, her cheek would press against his rough coat. And there would be a few tears. Undoubtedly there would be a few tears, which he, with gentle words and just a little banter, would wipe away with his own manly handkerchief. "There! There!"

He glanced at his watch. She had been gone twenty minutes, and at any moment she might return. There was a tap at the door. Could it be . . . ? No, it was the liftman.

"You're wanted on the telephone, sir."

"Ah, yes," murmured Heywood.

With the smirk of forgiveness already on his lips he followed the liftman downstairs.

His hand trembled as he raised the receiver to his ear.

"Hullo?"

"Is that Mr Heywood?"

"Yes," he answered. But he was very careful to keep his satisfaction out of his voice.

There is a time for everything, and he would be tender enough when his moment came. But a man had his dignity to think of, and a little preliminary coolness would do Pauline no harm.

"Oh, is that you, Tommy? It's Pauline speaking."

"Yes." He spoke reassuringly, for there was something, after all, devilish pathetic in her situation. "Yes, my dear."

"Oh, Tommy," said Pauline, "I want you to have my trunk sent back at once. Will you, please?"

Heywood could hardly believe his ears. "Sent back? Sent back where?"

"Why, sent back home, of course. And please don't forget to write a new label for it. Will you do this for me, Tommy? Promise."

"Yes, but . . ."

"You do promise?"

"Yes, but I say . . ."

He heard a little click. There was a long silence. And then a voice, a new voice, spoke suddenly into his ear: "Number, please?"

From "The World in Bud"

THE WORLD IN BUD

WHEN Sheila Dyrle came down to breakfast
Mr Pappin twittered, with benevolent
unction : " Happy little girl ! If only *I* were six
years old ! " Not that it was Sheila's birthday :
that event was already three months past. But
now it almost seemed to Sheila that every day
might have been a birthday, so full had her world
become of new and pleasant things. This house
was so utterly different from the house which,
since her father's death, had been home to her.
The rooms were shabby and small, their walls
copiously beflowered, the furniture swathed in
cretonne. The pictures, too, were of a different
kind—a much brighter, glossier kind than those
in Aunt Hester's house. Strangest of all, there
was a cupboard under the stairs that was full
of dusty old toys : Edgar's toys, Mrs Pappin
said, but if you asked her who Edgar was she
would never answer, though at all other times
she was talkative enough. Wandering along
the dark corridors you might at any moment
encounter one of those Paying Guests that
infested the large house ; and in the basement
there was a billiard-room where the strange
creatures met together to play games and smoke
and roar. They didn't take meals with their

host, for, as Mrs Pappin confided to Sheila, Mr Pappin had his position to think of, and it would never do to be too familiar; but Sheila found them attractive in a curious way, and she was not surprised to notice that sometimes, perhaps when he felt he had thought of his position long enough, Mr Pappin slipped downstairs to join the young men in a genteel roar. He himself, Mr Pappin, was not the least of Sheila's new delights. He was small, plump, bird-like, and a very knowing one. He was always telling you what chances he had nearly had, and how, if he had been in some people's place, or if some people had only had the wit to recognize certain qualities when they saw them in other people, " well, in *that* case, little lady, the dear wife here would have been able to take her rightful place in the world." To which Mrs Pappin would reply, with a tender smile: " To hear him talk, my dear, you'd think I was discontented. But believe me when I say there's not a prouder woman in the kingdom, *nor* out of it." Sheila believed her at once, though it was on the tip of her innocent tongue to ask: " Don't you mind him not being quite a gentleman ? " For she knew, having heard Aunt Hester mention it to Granny, that Mr Pappin was not quite a gentleman, was even (Aunt Hester said) a rather common little man. Aunt Hester, the grown-up second-cousin who was now Sheila's guardian, had never quite approved of this friendship with the Pappins;

194

and her disapproval made it the more surprising that she had ever consented to Sheila's accepting the invitation to stay at the house in Beechwood Road. The house was called " Sans Souci," which meant, one of the bigger girls at school had told her, that it was free of mice. Sheila was quick to urge this in its favour in pleading with Aunt Hester ; but it was another reason, and a very special one, that had finally turned the scale. That special reason was Granny, and when Sheila remembered Granny she felt it would be wicked to let Mr Pappin say " Happy little girl ! " without some sort of protest.

" I'm not really quite and altogether happy, you know," she said.

" Dear me ! Dear me ! " cried Mr Pappin. " And pray, why not ? "

He looked almost offended, so Sheila quickly answered : " Because of Granny. That's all."

" Ah ! " sighed Mr Pappin.

" Ah ! " echoed Mrs Pappin, turning up her eyes.

Man and wife exchanged a glance of mournful satisfaction ; and Sheila, intercepting it, couldn't resist the conviction that Granny, in being about to die, was doing something very grand and creditable. She felt suddenly proud of Granny, and was almost reconciled to the loss of her, if the removal of so tremendous and mysterious a figure could be termed a loss. Granny had always commanded in Sheila more of awe than of affection. She was so immense, so taciturn, so immobile, that it was terrifying to conjecture what went on, what prodigious secret thoughts, behind that waxen mask, behind those dim, film-covered eyes. She spoke but rarely, and then, nearly always, with querulous impatience. To Aunt Hester's chatter she did not so much as listen; yet when Aunt Hester had a headache and could find nothing to talk about, the ancient woman did not fail to remark upon the fact with indignation and contempt. It was all very puzzling to Sheila, who could not begin to understand what made Granny so deeply displeased with life, unless it were that she was offended at not having been invited to heaven sooner. If that was the trouble it was likely to be removed at any moment; or so Sheila, by putting two and two together, surmised. God, who had already taken Sheila's father, to say nothing of her mother, whom she could not remember at all clearly, now required Granny as well to keep Him company, being, as it seemed, never satisfied, and singularly without relations of His own. Riding to heaven in a glass carriage drawn by black horses, that was the process called dying; and, whatever it might be for the dead, she knew by bitter experience that it was very poor fun for those left behind. On this occasion she couldn't help wondering, very privately, if God quite knew what He was in for with poor Granny. That was Aunt Hester's phrase, "poor Granny," and its use, being unprecedented, had told Sheila, even more eloquently than Bella the maid's pregnant " Eh, she'll be away this time, Miss Sheila ! " that some big and terrible thing was about to happen to Granny.

But it did not happen quickly. Sheila had already spent three weeks of her summer holidays with the Pappins, and she could now scarcely believe that home, Aunt Hester's house, was only a quarter of an hour's walk away. In her mind it was nothing but a bright distant picture, renewed for her once a week by Aunt Hester's visit, a picture into which, in moments of reverie, she sometimes moved, revisiting past scenes and discovering familiar objects with a queer little thrill of recognition. This introspective world was part of Sheila ; it was, so to speak, seated at the breakfast-table now, receiving into itself the exotic Mr Pappin, his plump red face, his blue eyes, his asthma, his audible mastication of eggs and bacon, and his thrilling allusions to that great, that secret world of affairs in which he might have been, had this and that fallen out differently, a veritable king.

Mr Pappin had a way of making everything he said seem at once weighty and romantic. " There's a letter this morning, my dear," he said to his wife, fixing her with a profound stare.

" A letter ? " echoed Mrs Pappin. Her eyes widened.

Mr Pappin leaned slightly towards her across

the table, his little fat stomach pressed against its edge. " My dear," said he . . . and after a dramatic pause he added—almost in a whisper : " A letter."

" Is it," ventured Mrs Pappin, " from a certain person you was telling me of ? "

Mr Pappin braced himself to the task of revelation. His stare became more intense, more significant. Then with the air of one who throws discretion to the winds, he said deliberately : " It is from Colonel Bunch himself."

Colonel Bunch ! For Sheila the name was pure magic, like Sinbad the Sailor or a man out of the Bible. Colonel Bunch, whom she had never seen, was known to her as the mysterious agent of Mr Pappin's future aggrandizement. Hints had been dropped, small seeds that blossomed excitingly. The Colonel recognized capacity when he saw it. The Colonel, awful in power and god-like in benevolence, was even at this moment—so she had gathered from certain nods and smiles and portentous pursings of lips —secretly engaged in putting Mr Pappin in the way of a good thing. She was consumed with a desire to know what that good thing could be. On her plate was a fascinating little lake of milk surrounded by an island of porridge, which in its turn was surrounded by more milk. For the past few moments Sheila had been busy irrigating this island, constructing canals with her spoon from the still lake in the middle to the tossing sea at the circumference. Three of these canals were in working order; the construction of the fourth was interrupted by her glancing up, full of this new excitement, to watch the wonderful letter being passed across the table. Mrs Pappin, in the act of adjusting her spectacles, became aware of Sheila's scrutiny and said: "Now then! Eat your breakfast, ducky, like a good girl. And when you've finished you can run into the garden and play." Reluctant to destroy her island of porridge, still more reluctant to miss the least pulse of the joyous agitation that she could feel vibrating around her, she yet could do nothing but obey. Mrs Pappin was kind but firm, sometimes more firm than kind. Once or twice Sheila had been obscurely aware that Mrs Pappin resented her presence because she was not Edgar, and because, being a little girl, she could not very plausibly even pretend to be Edgar. And now Mrs Pappin was watching to see her command carried out.

II

The garden here was smaller than Aunt Hester's, and its fence so high that you couldn't hope to see over it except from the shoulders of a Paying Guest. From that elevation other people's backyards were visible: on the one side the Marvells, on the other side the Seccombes, and at the back the numerous Glovers. Mrs Marvell's husband was High Church, and Mr Seccombe's wife was French, and didn't mind what she said; so as neighbours these two families hardly existed. Fortunately they knew their place, said Mrs Pappin, and were quiet. The trouble about the Glovers, on the other hand, was that they existed too audibly. There were seven children; the eldest was eleven, and they were all dirty and noisy. Even when you couldn't hear them, you could, declared Mrs Pappin, smell them. Mrs Glover was a tall thin woman, with four cart-ruts across her forehead; Mr Glover was rather plump, with putty-coloured cheeks, and black hair that fell in ringlets round his bald buttered crown; and they had both smiled at Sheila when one day, balancing on Mr Hake's shoulder, she happened to encounter their gaze.

The Pappins' garden contained no flowers, but it did, luckily and surprisingly, contain a tree, a shabby, unclimbable, but wonderful tree, to the trunk of which was fastened one end of the clothes-line. To this tree Sheila ran, hoping, hoping ardently, that the lovely green bird had come to visit her again. Never had she seen such a bird before, and the sight of him sitting on the highest branch of this solitary tree had been for her like something out of a fairy-tale. The tree was tame, dowdy, domesticated; shorn of its lower branches, sooted by a hundred chimney-pots; its trunk positively polished by the rub of human hands. Yet in this tree, miraculously poised upon its topmost twig, had perched the gay bird, dainty and debonair,

incredible epitome of green fields and running
water, sunlight and the pulsing magic of summer.
He was elegant and sleek, satin-feathered in
golden green, a very prince of beauty. Whence
he had come, and why, was all a matter for
dazzling conjecture. Indeed, he was gone
almost before Sheila could ask herself the
question; and, every day since, she had scattered
crumbs on the black trampled ground in the
hope of coaxing him back. But no, he would
not be tempted; he had not come again, and
this morning, with the bird denied her, and the
secret of Colonel Bunch dangled before her eyes
and then withdrawn, Sheila felt a trifle dismal.
She wished something would happen.

" Hullo, Jane ! " cried a voice behind her.

It was her friend Mr Hake. She turned to
confront him frowningly, pretending to be cross.
" My name's *not* Jane ! " she declared, stamping
her foot. " How many times am I to tell you ! "
Mr Hake seemed so profoundly delighted by
this remark that she repeated it out of sheer
kindness of heart, and joined in his laughter.
He could enjoy a joke, this Mr Hake, but he was
not greatly given to laughter. Half the secret
of Sheila's affection for him lay in that fact.
He could always be relied upon to listen atten-
tively to her views on life, and to discuss them
with becoming seriousness, as man to man. The
world is full of delightful and funny things;
and Mr Hake's idea of what was delightful,
and what was funny, and what could be taken

7*

for granted and called for no comment at all, coincided with Sheila's to a degree that made for firm friendship. But, more than this, he was a singularly gifted man : he could move his eyebrows, one up and one down, like a see-saw ; and on Mondays, Wednesdays, and Fridays, though not (as he explained) on other days, he could suck his cheeks in and make the noise of a clucking hen. He had black side-whiskers and a blue chin, and one of his teeth was crowned with gold. On the lapel of his jacket he wore a little badge in the form of two masculine and amicably clasped hands.

"And what were you expecting to find in that tree ? " asked Mr Hake. "The bird of paradise ? "

Wonderful how he knew things without being told ! Sheila only hoped that she herself, when she was twenty-five like him, would be half as clever as Mr Hake. "Yes, he's a greeny goldy bird, and he came here to see me on Tuesday. I've put crumbs out every day, but he won't come back. A goldy greeny bird he is."

"A yellow-hammer," said Mr Hake. "Did he go like this ? " Mr Hake doubled himself up and pretended to ruffle his tail-feathers.

"No, he didn't," Sheila told him. "He just sat on the twig, quite still. And the next moment he was gone."

"Then he *must* have been a yellow-hammer," declared Mr Hake, resuming his humanity.

202

" Because any other bird would certainly have done that. And this, too," he added. The eyebrows came into play.

" Oh, Mr Hake," cried Sheila, clasping her hands together in admiration, " aren't you *glad* you can twizzle your eyebrows ? "

" Ah," responded that accomplished man, " but I can wag my ears too. Watch me now ! "

Mr Hake thrust forward his face so that his head, which had always seemed to Sheila to be a detachable object resting on a high stiff collar, was seen to be attached to his body by a long leathery neck. He inflated his cheeks like the frog in the fable ; and gradually he grew very red. Sheila watched the performance with the liveliest interest. Unable to speak, he made frantic gestures to indicate that she must stare not at his eyes but at his ears.

" Well ? " said Mr Hake, when he felt equal to speech, " what do you think of that ? "

" It was lovely," answered Sheila politely. " Of course they didn't *quite* wag, did they ? But it must be awfully difficult."

Mr Hake smiled sadly. " I'm broken-hearted. You cruel, cruel woman ! My heart is at your feet, and you trample on it. Now it's my belief," said Mr Hake, wagging a reproachful forefinger at her, " it's my belief that you've got your eye on yonder Colonel."

" Colonel Bunch ! " Sheila smiled happily.

" That very same. And a fine fellow he is, my dear Lady Jane. You'll like him ; he's got a pair of moustaches that 'ud make any woman like him. And he twirls them, let me tell you. 'Might I ask,' says he, 'if you can direct me to the house of Mr Pappin?' And when I brought him into the house he shook me by the hand and said : 'Thanks very much, old boy!' A friendly fellow, Colonel Bunch. As for your yellow-hammer, Lady Jane—if you'll find a spade for me I'll soon fetch him back."

"There's a spade," said Sheila, pointing. "Over there!" She ran to fetch it, and returned dragging it behind her. "Now what are you going to do, Mr Hake?"

"I'm going to dig up a bit of this ground." He grasped the spade, planted a foot on it, and pushed and grunted. "My, this is hard ground! It's like Mrs Pappin's pastry. No, I didn't mean that," he added hastily. "Forget it, Jane. Mrs Pappin makes very nice pastry, doesn't she? My dentist loves it."

"But what are you digging a hole for?" asked Sheila.

"Constancy rewarded!" remarked Mr Hake, flinging down his spade. "There, look at that!"

"It's only a little hole."

Mr Hake, with a comic groan, set to work once more. "If you want to know," said he, "I'm digging for worms. This newly turned earth, my dear, will attract Master Yellow-hammer. He'll come in search of worms. Crumbs are all very well in their way, but now and again a fellow likes a scrap of meat to go with his bread. He does indeed!" sighed Mr Hake wistfully.

"Lunch is ready, sir!"

A depressed female child stood in the kitchen doorway—Netty, the Pappins' maid-of-all-work. Mr Hake flung down his spade with a certain eagerness, and Sheila followed him into the house. There they parted; he to his own place, she to the family dining-room. Secretly she had longed, in the past, to be allowed to share meals with Paying Guests, so that she might study at close quarters the habits of that eccentric race; but to-day she was eager to sit at the Pappins' board, being only too willing to exchange Mr Hake for the mere possibility of Colonel Bunch.

And here he was, larger than life, the most surprising personage that Sheila had ever seen. To the Colonel's moustache Mr Hake had done no more than justice. That it was long and copious was but a trifle: its peculiar and hideous distinction, in Sheila's eyes, was that it gushed, reddish brown, not only from his upper lip, but from his large exposed nostrils. It gushed angrily, drooped like a pair of red tusks for five inches, and then was decisively twirled up. The Colonel himself did his best to be worthy of this magnificent appendage. He wore a bold check suit and a pepper-coloured waistcoat with leather buttons. His face was red, with a redness that made Mr Pappin's rosy cheeks seem pale ; and his large expanse of nose was decorated by a network of minute purple veins. Sheila faltered in the doorway ; and the Colonel, catching sight of her, allowed his sentence to die in its prime and his jaw to remain slightly and protestingly open. His bulging eyes glared question.

"Come along, ducky," said Mrs Pappin. "The Colonel won't eat you."

Sheila shyly responded : "Won't he ?"

The Colonel's body shook ; at first silently, but gradually the motion appeared to generate sound in him, and Sheila, watching, was aware of the gathering storm, which finally, after rumbling and rattling inside him for a few seconds, emerged as a shout of laughter. She thought, to herself, gravely, that the eruption of Vesuvius, of which Aunt Hester had told her a wonderful tale, must have been something like that ; and she couldn't but stare at the prodigy. The Colonel, however, quickly forgot her ; his mirth subsided.

"And I take this opportunity of saying, Mrs Pappin," said the Colonel, drawing up his chair to the luncheon-table, "that my instinct is seldom at fault, madam."

Mrs Pappin glowed at him. "Ah, there's not much, I dare say, as escapes your eye, Colonel."

"You may say so, Mrs Pappin," the Colonel assured her. "Though not one to boast, I'll confess that I am something of a judge of character. And when I first saw your good husband I knew the kind of man he was. Nothing personal, Mrs Pappin, but I knew that he was an *unusual* man, a man that would make his mark in the world. I'm not a scholar, madam, nothing of the kind. But I'm a thinker, if you see what I mean. And I can see at a glance that you're a thinker yourself, so you'll understand, where others perhaps wouldn't, when I say that I took an interest in your husband. Seeing him there in the private bar of the hotel—or public-house, as you might say, for hard words break no bones—seeing him there enjoying his glass, and not ashamed of it neither, I said to myself: ' Here's no ordinary man,' I said. ' He's a bit of a caution, he is,' if you'll pardon me, Mrs Pappin, ' and I'd like to know more of him,' I said. ' There's something about his eyes, something in the way he carries himself,' I said, ' that suggests to me . . .' Well, I won't deceive you, Mrs Pappin. ' Genius ' was the word that come into my mind. I may have been wrong, madam, but that was the word I wanted."

Sheila noticed that Mr Pappin was blushing rosily, and fluttering, and pecking nervously with his fork at the food on his plate, more like a little bird than ever. He was moved to protest. " Oh come, Colonel ! "

The Colonel raised his hand. " Allow me, Pappin ! Your good wife and I are having a little chat together about a certain gentleman we know. Nothing to do with you, my dear fellow, nothing at all. Mrs Pappin and I understand one another. Ha, ha, ha!" He laughed again, and the table shuddered under the shock. "From that moment, Mrs Pappin, my mind was made up. My name's not Parker and never has been, but I'm not above taking an interest. We got talking, me and your good husband, and it's not too much to say that I drew Mr Pappin out. 'They call me Colonel Bunch,' I said, 'but I'm not an army man and I'll not pretend I am. Everything fair and square and above-board,' I said; and those were my very words, Mrs Pappin." He turned sharply on her husband. "Isn't that so, old friend?"

Mr Pappin, in a voice trembling with emotion, declared that it was so. He made the declaration almost fiercely, as though challenging denial; and the two men nodded at each other, grunted, and suddenly rose to their feet and clasped hands across the table. It was all so dramatic, and so satisfying, that Sheila could hardly refrain from clapping and asking them to do it again. If she did not do so it was only because she felt herself to be within an ace of hearing all about that "good thing" which the Colonel was putting Mr Pappin in the way of. After this heroic preamble there was much deep talk between the men, with Mrs Pappin, apparently content to be left out of it, audibly breathing benediction upon them in a series of joyous sighs; and, while its purport was not at all clear to Sheila, she did manage to extricate the fact that the good thing was at the disposal of a gentleman called Sir Perceval Mountain, M.P.

" And if I say the word to Sir Perceval," remarked Colonel Bunch, with a kind of gloomy pride, " he'll think as I do, Mr Pappin, that you're the man for the job. Now could you be there Monday, d'ye think? Monday night, eh, ah pars eight? "

" At the door? " inquired Mr Pappin with a shrewd look.

" At the door it is," replied the Colonel.

" Of the Stroud Green Empire itself, of course? " said Mr Pappin, who seemed, Sheila thought, as eager to have it all clear as she herself was.

" *At* the door," said Colonel Bunch, " *of* the Empire. You take me, Mr Pappin? "

" I take you, Colonel."

" And, of course," said the Colonel, in an off-hand way, " spruce and spry, as it goes without saying. A nice white shirt! " He stroked his chest illustratively. " A nice tail-coat." He half rose, then reseated himself, after adjusting imaginary coat-tails. " Smart and ship-shape, that's the ticket. No need to tell you that."

Sheila was instantly aware of a change in the emotional temperature. The Pappins' reception of this last piece of advice may have deceived Colonel Bunch, but it didn't deceive her. She could see at once that they were agitated; their enthusiasm had received a check . . . And at odd times during the afternoon, when there was nothing better to do, she pondered this mystery. The Colonel went away as soon as lunch was over, and not until, bereaved of his magnificence, the Pappins and Sheila reassembled for tea, was anything more said in her hearing about Monday night, and the Empire, and being smart and ship-shape.

"Of course," said Mrs Pappin, "there's ways of managing. F'rinstance, they *can* be hired."

"M . . . yes." Mr Pappin seemed reluctant to embrace this possibility. His eyes were wistful with a vision of splendour. "But don't you see," he argued, "one would want it constantly, night after night, from week's end to week's end, if what we hoped for took place. A manager's a manager, music-hall or no music-hall. And then we should *have* to purchase, and forfeit the hire money, as I see it. Of course, if what we hope for doesn't take place . . ."

"Ah! don't suggest it!" interposed Mrs Pappin. "We've the Colonel's word—and who should know better, them being old school-fellows together!—we've the Colonel's word for it that Sir Perceval Mountain, M.P., is looking for just the man you are."

"Of course," conceded Mr Pappin, "we could *try* hiring . . ."

But his wife cried impulsively: "No, we'll buy. We'll buy." Sheila could see, and she knew Mrs Pappin could see, that more than anything else, more even than the good thing promised him by the Colonel, Mr Pappin desired just now to possess this treasure of which they were talking. He was intoxicated with the idea. Already, as the light in his eyes betrayed, he saw it as his own, saw himself the proud master of it; Sheila knew the feeling well. And a reflection of that same light shone in the glance with which Mrs Pappin reassured him. "We'll buy," she repeated firmly. "My little something that I've put away—that'll pay for it and a bit over!" Sheila was still not quite sure what it was they were to buy, but she could tell that the decision was a momentous one. The atmosphere was electric with happiness. Sheila herself was so happy, so sharply aware that a small new joy had just been born to her childless friends that she wanted to weep and sing when Mrs Pappin finally disposed of the matter by saying: "This very afternoon I'll see about drawing out the money. And to-morrow we'll do our bit of shopping together."

III

The yellow-hammer was slow in returning. Five days went by; Saturday came; and not even cake-crumbs, not even the most luscious worms, had availed to lure the bird back. This disappointment, combined with others, invested the backyard with something of melancholy.

The complete absence of vegetation, except the tree, was undeniably a disadvantage; the noises made by the dirty little Glovers playing on the other side of the high fence afforded tantalizing hints of companionship; and Sheila more than once caught herself wishing that she could exchange this black oblong of earth, these rumours of fun, for Aunt Hester's little garden with its prim flowers and its vista of railway. For now the first excitement of her visit had passed. The Pappins had in effect withdrawn themselves from her into their private adventure, of which, in her mind, Colonel Bunch, that vanished and by now almost mythical creature, was the symbol; and even her Chubblers, a family of friendly little animals invented by herself and obedient to her every whim, held less interest for her now than formerly. She looked forward with increasing pleasure to Mr Hake's daily appearances. With him she had some trifle of conversation every day when he came home to lunch. The afternoons she spent, with such toys as she had with her, in the spare bedroom that overlooked the street.

It was from the window of this room that she witnessed a ceremony which she recognized, after an instant's awed speculation, as Granny's ride to heaven. The glass carriage, filled with white flowers, was drawn by four long-tailed black horses. Two waxworks gentlemen in tall silk hats sat in front, one on each side of the driver; and two others stood, stiff and straight,

on a little ledge at the back, with their fingers
resting primly on the edge of the glass frame as
though they were about to play a pianoforte
duet. All four looked proud and miserable and
somehow cruel. In the first of the three carriages
that followed, Sheila caught sight of Aunt
Hester, dressed in black and weeping, and—
could it be possible?—at Aunt Hester's side sat
Uncle Peter. For a moment Sheila could hardly
refrain from pushing up the window and calling
out a greeting to Uncle Peter. But something in
the aspect of this procession intimidated her. In
all respects save one it fulfilled her imagination
of what this great event, this departure for the
City of God, should have been. But there was
one thing missing; for one face she looked in
vain. This, she had supposed, was Granny's
great day. Where then was Granny? She could
see no sign of her. In a glass carriage, Bella
(Aunt Hester's maid) had told her; but this
glass carriage contained nothing except a long
brown box almost hidden by the white flowers.
Where was Granny? The question became an
urgent one; suddenly—for no reason that she
could understand—it was the most urgent
question she had ever asked herself, and until
it should be answered the sunshine was a glittering unreality, the sky a staring and empty face.
By now the procession had trailed slowly out
of sight; but Sheila had not forgotten that long
brown box, and a queer conjecture crept into
her mind and gripped her young limbs in a kind

of paralysis. When, presently, a hand fell gently upon her head, she uttered a gasp of terror and stumbled forward on to her knees, hiding her face in her hands, afraid to look round.

"It's only me, ducky. It's only Auntie Pappin." Sheila made no response. "Lord, I'm ashamed!" declared Mrs Pappin. "As nice a funeral as you could wish, and me with all the blinds up!"

Sheila squirmed round, uncovered her small blanched face, and demanded: "Where's my Granny?"

"Ah, she's gone, poor lady!" said Mrs Pappin, smacking her lips mournfully. "But don't take it to heart, child. It was only what you might expect at her age."

To this generalization Sheila paid no heed. "What have they done to her?"

She was dry-eyed, rigid, accusing. Mrs Pappin's glance faltered under that steady inquisitory gaze. "Come, ducky!" she said. "Mr Pappin's new suit's arrived. We've laid it out on the bed and very nice it looks, I *must* say. If you're a good girl I'll take and show it to you."

Hand in hand, making believe to have forgotten all about Granny, Sheila and Mrs Pappin set out in search of the nice new suit, most of which they found already attached to the person of Mr Pappin himself. Splendid in his dress shirt and collar, heroic in a waistcoat from which his stomach struggled to escape, Mr Pappin greeted them cordially at the bedroom door.

"Well, Father," said Mrs Pappin, "I've brought little Shelia to see you in your finery. How do you feel now?"

"So so!" replied Mr Pappin, in a self-conscious, off-hand way. "It's a *leetle* tight, perhaps, in the region of the—ah—bread-basket, as they say. But I fancy it'll do, my love." Whistling unmelodiously through his teeth, he turned to the bed across which lay the new coat. With his wife's help he tried the coat on. "How does it fit on the shoulders?" he asked her, screwing his neck round in an endeavour to see for himself. He wriggled his arms, stared from all angles at his reflection in the wardrobe mirror, and patted and stroked himself at intervals. "Well, that's that!" he remarked at length, and his manner suddenly became rather bored, as though he grudged the time given to such a tiresome commonplace business as trying on a dress suit. A man in his position had to do such things; but the sooner it was over the better.

Mrs Pappin, loyally taking her cue from him, extinguished her fond maternal smile and said with an air of proud indifference: "Were you thinking of trying the tie on, Father?"

"H'm!" reflected Mr Pappin. He seemed doubtful whether he could bring himself to make this concession. "Well, there's no chance of *that* not fitting, after all." He laughed grimly.

"Don't bother," said Mrs Pappin, "if you're too busy."

He appeared to hesitate. "Well, if it'll please the little lady here . . ."

Sheila knew, though she knew not why, that it was an anxious moment for him. She said: "Oo yes, please, Mr Pappin!"

"I think it would be nice, Father," ventured Mrs Pappin. "It won't take a minute."

"Very well!" said he. Slightly, and not unkindly, he shrugged his shoulders. The stern fellow was relenting. He was generously allowing himself to be persuaded. Mrs Pappin approached him, white tie in hand. With a laugh he submitted to her ministrations. "Ah, you women!" he exclaimed teasingly. But he couldn't any longer keep the happiness out of his voice, the dancing excitement out of his eyes. Catching Sheila's grave interested stare, he almost blushed, like a boy.

IV

"*At* the door *of* the Empire!" murmured Sheila to her porridge on Monday morning. But the remark was not well received, and she quickly learned that the coming event loomed so large already in the Pappins' imagination that they could not suffer the least reference to it. Why this should be she did not understand, for she herself was in the habit, when the mood took her, of talking incessantly of all pleasures, past, present, and to come. Knowing herself excluded from her friends' confidence, seeing them shut away from her in a world of unimaginable adultness, she felt more than ever forlorn, and her thoughts, as she wandered disconsolately from playroom to yard, yard to kitchen, kitchen to billiard-room—whence she was shoo'd away by Netty, the little servant girl—turned more and more into herself, into the world of Aunt Hester, the house at Penlington, and Granny. (Ah, what had become of Granny?) Notwithstanding her excitement at seeing Mr Pappin go forth in his new suit to that marvellous meeting with Colonel Bunch, Sheila—as she climbed, clinging to Netty's hand, the stairs to her bedroom—could think of little but Granny, and Granny's mysterious fate.

When she was tucked up she asked: "Netty, do *you* know where my Granny is?"

Netty made big eyes at her and sniffed noisily. She seemed to be shocked by the question. "Your Granny? Why, she's . . . gorn."

"But where?" asked Sheila. "And why didn't I see her in the glass carriage?"

"She's gorn," reiterated Netty. She sniffed. "Gorn . . . alorft," she added. The phrase seemed to afford her a certain pleasure. "And now you must go bye-byes. See?"

She sniffed again, triumphantly, and withdrew, taking the candle with her. Left alone, glad to be released from the torment of that sniffing,

Sheila soon fell asleep . . . and here was Netty back again, saying " Time to get up ! " and the room was full of morning sunshine. She sprang out of bed at once, although she knew by the odour of sleep that hung about Netty, and by her drowsy unwashed appearance, that it was not really time to get up at all. But Sheila was eager enough to begin the day. For her the world was made new every morning, and the dark thoughts and strange surmises that had troubled her overnight were all, for the moment, forgotten.

" It's nice and early, isn't it ? " she asked Netty.

" Nasty and early, I call it ! " declared Netty, with a sniff more truculent than usual. " But *they're* getting up already. Something biting 'em, if you ask *me*. They came and called me theirselves, 'arf an hour too early."

" Colonel Bunch ! " exclaimed Sheila, half to herself. It had become her fixed belief that anything unusual that occurred in the Pappin household could be explained in terms of Colonel Bunch. " Oh, how lovely ! " she said. For this happy event, this unwonted early rising, could have but one meaning for her mind : that the expected good thing, in quest of which Mr Pappin had gone to meet the Colonel last night, was now in her friends' possession. She was impatient to finish her dressing so that she might run downstairs and take part in the family rejoicing.

But the breakfast-room was empty. She lingered for a few minutes ; then, vaguely disappointed, she wandered out into the passage, through the kitchen, and so to the backyard. This morning the little place wore for her an unaccustomed brightness. The air was fresh and warm ; the solitary tree seemed surprisingly to have recovered, in a single night, its green youth ; and it was as if the bare flowerless ground quivered in a kind of ecstasy under the flood of sunlight. And there at last, under the tree, was the yellow-hammer, come back to her after his long inconstancy. He was lying on the ground asleep. What a funny attitude to go to sleep in ! With silence in the heart she bent over him and stretched out timid fingers. The body was cold and stiff, the eyes glassily staring . . . and suddenly a question that was no longer a question burst like a thunderclap in her ears. Faces leered and voices screamed, a black pit opened at her feet, and the morning, so fresh and calm and bright, was a glittering mockery. Her universe crumbled and was dust.

Clutching the dead bird, she ran into the house in search of human comfort. At the door of the breakfast-room she heard Mr Pappin cry out in a strange voice : " My love, never mention that scoundrel to me again ! " But not for an instant was she distracted from her obsession. She burst into the room. Mr and Mrs Pappin sat facing each other across the table, naked

misery staring from their eyes.   Into the meaning
of that misery the little girl did not stop to probe.
She ran forward to Mrs Pappin, mutely extending
the hand that held the bird ; and at last, after an
inarticulate interval, she managed to say between
sobs : " Granny's *dead !* "

From " The World in Bud"

THE STREET OF THE EYE

B<small>Y</small> one of those fantastic coincidences that make life sometimes seem more artificial than fiction, as well as stranger (said Saunders), it was in a little *café* in Rue de l'Œil, Marseilles, that I first noticed Bellingham. Strange that one should have to journey to the south of France to make the acquaintance of a fellow-collegian! For Bellingham, too, was a Jesus man. I had nodded to him a hundred times in the Close, walked with him once or twice for a few hundred yards, and passed him every day in the Chimney going to or from lectures; but I knew next to nothing of him. Once, I remember, we met in the rooms of some other fellow and had coffee. Furnivall was there, who afterwards made something of a hit as an actor; Dodd who got a double first in classics, and then, before the results were out, accidentally drowned himself within sight of Trinity Library; Chambers who, under a Greek pseudonym, wrote donnish elderly witticisms for undergraduate journals. Looking back on that inauspicious scene I know that not one of the men I have named possessed half the spiritual force of Bellingham, and yet, had it not been for after-events, I should not now have remembered that

he was there at all. He was a tall slackly built
man, rather like a black sackful of unco-ordinated
bones ; he stooped a little, peering out at the
world under long bushy eyebrows from behind
a large nose. The mouth was large and loose ;
the cheeks sagged a trifle ; the ears stuck out
from the head at an angle that, if you looked
twice, seemed excessive ; and the hands were
big and bony with long fingers that moved,
sometimes, like a piece of murderous mechanism.
It was as if the hands of a strangler had been
grafted on to the body of a morose, ungainly
saint. I do not describe him as he appeared to
me in that college room : that would be impossible, for I simply didn't observe him. He was
no more to me then than an uninteresting ultra-
reserved fellow-student drudging at ecclesiastical
history and similar stuff. That I failed to single
him out is sufficiently amazing to me now. My
eyes must have been in my boots. But there it is
—he made no impression on my somnolent
mind. It was not, as I say, until we met again in
that little *café* in Rue de l'Œil that I really saw
Bellingham. For the thousandth time I looked
at him and for the first time I saw him. There was
quite a little crowd of us : Hayter of Caius ;
Mulroyd with his soft voice and Irish cadences ;
an Oxford man whose name I've forgotten ; and
the Honourable Somebody, a mild-mannered,
flaxen-haired boy, a Fabian socialist trying to
live down the fact that he was the younger son
of a peer. But I'm forgetting myself : these

people are merely names to you, and names they must remain. The Oxonian was a chance acquaintance who had encountered our party in Paris and diffidently joined us, a charming fellow who constantly tried—only too successfully, for he remains in my memory as the vaguest phantom —to efface himself. Hayter, whose chief pre-occupation, I remember, was the maturing of a new Meerschaum, played the elder brother to the flaxen-haired youngster. Mulroyd was my own particular friend, and it was he who had dragged in Bellingham, the misfit of the party. Belling-ham was a curiously solitary man, a ward in Chancery or something of the kind ; no one knew anything about his origin or antecedents, and he had no friends. The suspicion that he was lonely, neglected, with nowhere to spend the Long Vacation, made him irresistible to Mul-royd; and that he was conspicuously unsociable Mulroyd regarded as a clarion call of challenge to his own militant kindliness. Well, there's a rough sketch of the crowd that gathered in that little red-tiled, black-raftered, French hostel. You must imagine us all as sitting or standing about the place, in various negligent attitudes, drinking execrable *vin rouge*, and talking of routes and train-services and the comparative merits of ales. What turned the conversation towards more ultimate matters I cannot begin to remem-ber, but turn it did. I think it was our Oxonian who interpolated some gloomy observation that set us all thinking of a brooding, inscrutable

Destiny which for ever watched, with hard unblinking eyes, our trivial conviviality, listened, with infinite indifference, to our plans of to-day and to-morrow. The remark was succeeded by a pause that was almost a collective shudder, a pause in which, as it seemed to me, we all listened fixedly to our own heart-beats ticking away the handful of moments that divided us from an unknown eternity. You know what it is to be recalled suddenly, wantonly, to a sense of the immensities, to be aware that death, an invisible presence, is in your midst, to feel his lethal breath chilling the warmth of your idle joy. Even Madeleine, the daughter of the house, who had watched us hitherto with laughter in her dark eyes, and innocent invitation on her full lips, was conscious of the abrupt change of temperature. She understood not a word of our speech, but out of the corner of my eye I saw her hand make the sign of the cross and her lips move in prayer. Hayter, shockheaded, long and oval of face, ceased fingering his pipe and seemed lost in contemplation of its mellowing colour. A wistful light shone in Mulroyd's eyes. The Honourable Somebody—I can't recall his name—smiled and said "Um." In that pregnant moment during which we all sat peering over the edge of the unfathomable, questioning the unresponsive darkness, that monosyllable sounded like an incantation, a word mystical and potent. As for me, I looked from one face to the other, trying to read what was written there, and so my glance fell upon Bellingham. Fell and was arrested, for the face of Bellingham was a revelation. What it revealed is difficult to describe in cold prose; a musician could better express it in some moaning, unearthly phrase of music. It was as if there shone from that face not light but darkness, and as if over that head hovered a halo of dark fear, a crown of shuddering doom. The eyes flashed darkness, I say, and yet through them, as through sinister windows, I saw for one instant into the infinite distances of the soul behind them, the unimaginable and secret world in which the real Bellingham, the Bellingham whom none of us in that room had ever seen or approached, lived his isolated life. He was leaning forward, elbows on knees, his chin propped up in those gaunt skeleton hands that were several sizes too big for him. To me, who stood facing him, the effect was incredibly bizarre: it was for all the world as though some monster whose face was hidden from me was crouching at my feet offering the truncated head of Bellingham for my acceptance. The red-knuckled fingers formed a fitting cup for the grotesque sacrifice. I put the horrible fancy behind me and sought to regain a human view of that face. Gaunt and pallid, with high cheek-bones and burning eyes, it was a battle-ground of conflicting passions. But the natures and names of the passions I could only surmise. An ascetic and a voluptuary, perhaps, had fought in Bellingham, and his face was the neutral ground that their warfare had violated and laid waste. The merest conjecture, this, and it remained so, until it was proved to be false.

" It doesn't bear thinking of," remarked Hayter, " so it's best to avoid the thought. The animals are better off than we, by a long chalk."

" There's religion," said the flaxen-haired Fabian tentatively.

" Soothing syrup," Hayter murmured. " Religion doesn't face death : it only pretends it isn't there. Gateway to the larger life, and all that cant." Hayter was a very positive young man in his way.

Mulroyd tried to banter us back into a more comfortable humour. " Material for a first-rate shindy there. Now then, Saunders, speak up for your cloth, my boy ! "

" I shall, when I've got it," said I. A theological student does not care to talk shop in mixed company. I was shy of posing as a preacher, and not to be drawn.

" Well, if Saunders won't, I will."

The voice was harsh, and tense with emotion. It seemed to come out of the grave itself. We all stared at Bellingham, whom we had become accustomed to regard as almost incapable of contributing to a conversation. We waited. Hayter even forgot that work of chromatic art, his pipe.

" Death waits for every man," said Bellingham. " At any moment it may engulf us." The triteness of the sermon was redeemed by the person-

226

ality that blazed in the speaker. "And then . . ."
His voice trailed off into silence.

"And then?" inquired Hayter, with a politeness that I fancied covered a sneer.

"And then," said the man of doom, "we
shall find ourselves in the terrible presence of
God."

For once even the genial Mulroyd was stung
to sarcasm. "I must say, judging from your
tone, you don't seem to relish the prospect
much."

"Never mind what I relish," answered
Bellingham sternly. "In that hour you and I
will be judged. We shall be forced to look into
the eye that at this moment, and always, is looking
upon us."

There was an uncomfortable silence, as well
there might be. We had not reckoned upon
such an explosion of evangelical fervour, and
it embarrassed us as some flagrant breach of
manners would have done. Perhaps, heaven
help us, we regarded it as a flagrant breach of
manners. Bellingham was committing the
cardinal sin : he was taking something too
seriously.

"When I was a child," went on Bellingham,
without ruth, "I was told the story of a prisoner
condemned to solitary confinement. To this
punishment was added the further horror of
perpetual watching. A small hole was drilled in
the cell-door through which an eye never ceased
to peer at the prisoner. That was an allegory,

227

and I have never forgotten it. Even now, you fellows, we are being watched."

Some of us, I swear, looked round nervously, half expecting to catch sight of that vigilant eye. I, for my part, was angry. "That's not an allegory, Bellingham," I said. "It's a damned travesty. You conceive God to be a kind of Peeping Tom, with omnipotence added. I would rather be an atheist than believe that."

"Perhaps you would rather be an atheist," retorted Bellingham. "Perhaps I would rather be an atheist. But I can't be. Nor can you. Did any of you notice the name of the street?"

"Name of the street?" echoed someone. "What street?"

"This street," said Bellingham.

"We're not in a street. We're in a *café*," said Hayter truculently. "At least I thought so a moment ago. I begin to fancy we must be in a mission-hall."

At the moment no one could remember having noticed the name. "Well, I did notice it," said Bellingham. "It is the Street of the Eye."

Mulroyd shrugged his shoulders, a gesture plainly disdainful of this touch of melodrama.

"Well," said I, "what of it?" For the fellow's morbidity had spoiled my temper. I expected a night of bad dreams.

"The Street of the Eye," repeated Bellingham. "We're all in that street; every man born is in that street. And we shall never get out of it."

I believe some of us half-suspected that the

wine had gone to his head, though how such stuff could make any man tipsy was beyond understanding. He continued to irradiate gloom upon us from under his shaggy brows. Mulroyd, to create a diversion, held out his hands to Madeleine in mock appeal.

"Du vin, mademoiselle! Nous sommes bien chagrinés."

The girl's eyes brightened again. At the merest hint of a renewal of gaiety she rose, radiantly, as if from the dead.

"Let's have some champagne," Mulroyd suggested, "to take the taste of death out of our mouths."

"*Carpe diem*," murmured Hayter. "Trite. But the first and last word of wisdom."

"You can't escape that way," remarked Bellingham, sourly insistent.

But we could stand no more of Bellingham just then. Flinging courtesy to the winds we laughed and sang and shouted him down. "Death be damned!" cried Mulroyd, as we clinked glasses. Never was a toast drunk with more fervour.

II

You'll be surprised when I say that after this incident I got to know Bellingham better and to like him more. Strange as it may seem, he was not entirely without humour; and I fancied that he was the least bit ashamed of his outburst. The next day he went about like a dog in disgrace, feeling perhaps that everyone disliked him. Back he went into that shell of silence from which he had only once, and with such dramatic effect, emerged. He would never, I know, have gone back on the substance of his discourse; but, as he admitted to me afterwards, he very quickly began to doubt the wisdom of his method. Fellow-undergraduates were not to be frightened into conversion by the kind of revivalist rant he had treated us to. He began to feel woefully out of place in our company. Mulroyd, good fellow though he was, could not bring himself to make any warm overtures to one whom he now regarded as a religious maniac; on the surface he was breezy and friendly enough, but in his heart he knew that Bellingham must be reckoned among his failures, one who had failed to justify his ardent faith in the latent social value of every man. The others ignored him, though not pointedly, much as they had always done. My own attitude was different. I have, as you know, an insatiable curiosity about human nature— especially freaks of human nature, I'm afraid —and Bellingham had piqued that curiosity. I had repudiated his particular version of God as being nothing but an almighty Peeping Tom, and yet a weakness for peeping is my own besetting sin. All my life I have been a kind of amateur detective of the human soul. Moreover—though I don't stress this—I had more than a sneaking sympathy for the man. After all, we had something in common, something that none of the others of our party shared with us. We were both hoping to be ordained. In spite of myself I had to admire the colossal courage of his intervention in that argument, even while I disparaged its tone. In fine, for this reason and for that, I made rather a point of cultivating Bellingham's acquaintance from that day forth. And I had my reward. I really believe that to me he revealed a more human side of himself than anybody else ever caught sight of. Next term, back at college, he made a habit of strolling into my rooms at five minutes to ten, and very often we talked till the early hours of the morning about this and that. Sometimes he became reminiscent about his childhood. His earliest memories were of a grey suburban villa, with a black square patch in front and a black oblong patch behind, both called gardens. The square one was marked off from the road by hideous iron railings and an iron gate. Bellingham assured me that the pattern of those railings was branded on his retina ; and in an unwonted lapse from literalism he declared that it was a pattern designed in hell and executed in Bedlam. "Wherever I see it," he said passionately, under the influence of nothing more potent than black coffee, "wherever I see it—and it is all over South-East London—I recognize the mark of the beast, the signature of an incorrigible stupidity. The very smell of those railings is noisome." He was like that : ever ready to see material things as symbols of the unseen, and very prone—like many religionists—to confuse the symbol with the thing symbolized. In the sheer exuberance of his passion, whether of joy or disgust, he would make some wild exaggerated statement that no one was expected to take literally; and the next moment he himself would be taking it literally. If, for example, I had suggested to him that to talk of the smell of railings was a trifle fanciful, he would have been genuinely astonished. Whenever he loved or hated, rationality went to the winds. And he seems to have hated the home of his childhood pretty completely. The back garden, where he spent a good deal of his time, figured in his talk as if it were a plague spot, an evil blot upon the earth. If one is to believe his tale, this garden was always, in season and out, full of wet flapping underclothes hanging on a line. They used to lie in wait for him, he said, and smack him in the face: it was like being embraced by a slimy fish. He was glad, however, of the clothes-line posts; he used to climb them and swing from the cross-bars, and once or twice he pulled one of these posts out of its wooden socket in the ground and stared down at the minute wriggling monsters that scuttled about in that little twilit world. Another thing that gave him pleasure was the sight of a neighbouring church, aspiring towards the sky, the throne of God. These memories may well have derived much of their colour from imagination, for both his parents died before he was ten, and he then left the suburban villa to become the ward of his uncle Joseph. Joseph Bellingham appears to have been conspicuously unfitted for the delicate task of bringing up a sensitive, solitary, and already morbid child, although not a word against him would his nephew have admitted. Justly or unjustly I was disposed to believe that this Uncle Joseph had completed the dark work begun in Bellingham by his childish solitude and loveless home. For his parents, I should have told you, were lifeless, disillusioned people. I suspect they had never been happy or passionate lovers, and that they regarded their son's birth as one more penalty rather than as the desired fruit of their marriage. In some preposterous way (naturally Bellingham was reticent here) the man had sacrificed himself in marrying his wife—some fetish of " honour " perhaps—and of course, he spent the rest of his life hating her for it. This may or may not account for the fact that when I first got to know Bellingham he seemed extraordinarily insensitive, for a man of his temperament, to beauty. Not totally deficient—because even his hatred of a certain kind of iron railings implies some standard, however subconscious—but what sense of beauty he possessed had never been wakened : it manifested itself only in a series of dislikes. He had quite a devilish flair for seeing the most repulsive aspect of things. This was all in tune with his miserable theology. To the spiritual loveliness that radiates from the central figure of the New Testament—to that beacon he was

8*

as blind as he was deaf to the many golden pro-
mises of the religion of Christ. I do not mean
that he swerved by a hair's breadth from
orthodoxy; I mean that there was some subtle
twist in his temperament that made him accept
" the love of God " as a euphemism and " the
wrath of God " as a terrible reality. He thought
more about hell than about heaven, because he
had only seen beauty, whereas he had *felt*
ugliness. The one was an intellectual apprehension: the other was a perpetual experience. It
was evident to me, from what he did not say,
that he had never known love, and I wondered
what was in store for him.

But though with me he became more and
more unreserved, from all other fellows of his
class and education he drew farther away. There
was a spiritual uncouthness in him which pre-
vented his taking kindly to the harmless social
artificialities of academic life. As I told him—
and he admitted it good-humouredly—he would
have been more at home as chief medicine-man
to a tribe of barbarians. In some remote and
savage bush his niche awaited him. Even the
traditions of politeness he grew to despise. I
shocked him by admitting that I myself had more
than once got out of accepting an invitation to
breakfast or to coffee by feigning to be engaged
elsewhere. Bellingham would have said bluntly,
" No, thanks," and have left it at that. Courageous, no doubt, but it did not make for easy social
relations. He became more and more dissatisfied,

too, with the mild fashionable Anglicanism of our dean. Of his own religion sensationalism was the life-breath; and the worship of good form, the religion of all undergraduates, was in his eyes the most dangerous idolatry. No one was surprised when, having taken his degree with the rest of us, he abruptly left the University. Instead of being ordained he became just what I had chaffingly suggested, a medicine-man to a tribe of barbarians. To be more exact, he set up as a lay-missioner near the Euston Road. He had a meagre but sufficient private income which permitted him to go his own solitary gait. And there he busied himself wrestling with the Devil for the souls of all the miscellaneous street-scum he could lay hands on. God forgive me if I have ever in my heart derided Bellingham! He had the heroism as well as the mania of a one-idea'd man. I find it hard to suppose that his converts were any the happier for having been injected with his particular virus of fear; but, as Bellingham would say, where happiness cannot be reconciled to salvation happiness must go. Go it did, I have no doubt. Fear of the police-man was displaced by a scarcely less ignoble fear of God, conceived to be another policeman on a much larger scale. If I speak bitterly, it is not in spite of my religion, but because of it. Before I have finished the story you will understand that I have cause for bitterness.

We exchanged a few letters, he and I; but it was not until eighteen months later that, at his own invitation, I went to see him. " Saunders, I need your help," he said in his letter, and added something about my being his only real friend and so on. He had dismal little lodgings in a dismal little side-street the name of which I have forgotten. Bellingham himself opened the door to me. I had told him when to expect me and he must have been waiting at the window. He greeted me in a shamefaced eager fashion that touched my heart. I was astonished at the change in him : the more astonished because it was at once subtle and impossible to miss. There was a gentleness in his eyes that I had never seen there before. He was more human. He led me to his own rooms—they were at the top of a four-storied house, and looked out on a prospect of smoking chimneys—and forced me into the only comfortable chair he possessed.

I began smoking, but he denied himself that nerve-soothing indulgence. His eyes, alight with an unwonted shyness that was only half-shame, avoided meeting mine. We fenced for a while, talking over our Jesus days ; and all the while my mind, involuntarily, was seeking a name for something in that room that I had not expected to find. Presently Bellingham rose from his chair. It was an abrupt and surprising movement. " Like to see the rest of my quarters ? " he said, in a tone desperately casual. I followed him into the next room, and there, in one glance, the mystery was made clear. The bedroom was the answer to the problem of the sitting-room. What I had detected while we sat talking was domesticity, a subtle but decided fragrance of home : a certain precision in the arrangement of books and furniture. In the bedroom, with its two spotlessly white-sheeted beds and its vase of flowers standing in the centre of a miniature dressing-table, the same story was told more eloquently ; there was, accentuated, aggressive, the same neatness and daintiness of effect which a contented woman instinctively imposes on her surroundings. No bachelor, however fastidious, could have achieved it. " Quite a jolly little place," I remarked, to hide my own surprise and his embarrassment. "Very," said Bellingham, and we went back to our seats by the fire.

Bellingham tried to take up the thread of our conversation where we had dropped it five minutes before. But for his own sake I cut off that line of retreat.

" Look here, my dear fellow ! You didn't ask me over here in order to discuss our esteemed Dr Morgan. Tell me all about it."

Bellingham faced me squarely at last. " You mean my marriage ? " I nodded. " Well, to start with, I'm not married."

I think he expected me to flinch at that ; and perhaps my failure to do so disconcerted as well as encouraged him. I said nothing. I felt that I could do more good by listening than by talking.

" She has been in these rooms for two months,"

said Bellingham. "And what you saw in there
—that has existed for ten days, just ten days."
I divined that this was his way of indicating to
me the duration of his married life. "You see
I didn't fall at once, or easily. The Devil is
always insidious, isn't he? Saunders, that girl
is a magician. Joan, her name is. She trans-
formed this place. It's not bad now, is it?
You should have seen it before she came. And
me, too—you should have seen me before she
came. It's a new life to me. I'm translated.
And yet . . ."

"How and where did you meet her?"

"In the street, at the beginning of November.
Her husband kicked her out. A swine he is;
thank God I've never set eyes on him. Told
her to go and sell herself, and come back with
her earnings."

There was a pause. "And she?" I asked.

"She was on the streets for five days. Yes,
a prostitute for five days." I saw Bellingham's
face contract with pain, and I knew that something deeper than pity had been stirred in him.
And so the recital went on. Bit by bit I got his
story and pieced it together. He did not spare
himself; but even his passion for repentance,
his ingrained conviction of sin, could not
persuade me that he had been guilty of a very
heinous crime. He had rescued the girl at first
in sheer compassion, and cherished her as he
would have cherished any other fragment of
human salvage. And her presence, her pathetic

238

prettiness and her childish need of affection, had been too much for him. In a passion of gratitude, I surmise, she had offered him, with a full heart, what she had so reluctantly sold to casual men during her five days' purgatory. The appeal to his manhood was too sudden, too overwhelming, to be resisted. Beauty, seen for the first time in dazzling glory, had invaded his heart and beaten down his defences. For the first time in my experience of him there was inconsistency in Bellingham. He spoke, one minute, of his " fall," like any sour moralist! and in his very next sentence he would become almost lyrical about this " new life," this shattering apocalypse of beauty. It was as if the man had been cloven in twain and spoke with two voices. And that, I believe, is the real key to the baffling terror that was to follow.

Later in the afternoon, in time to prepare tea for us, came Joan herself, a big-eyed child in her early 'twenties, with very fair hair, like a little lost angel with a Cockney accent. The sudden fear that leaped into her eyes as she timidly greeted me would have stabbed any man's heart. She was absurdly fragile, and I saw at once that those five evil days had been no more than a gruesome physical accident which had left her courage shaken but her innocence unimpaired. She guessed, no doubt, that we had been discussing her ; and both Bellingham and I felt caddish, I dare say, when we remembered having done so. But I succeeded in winning her confidence by displaying a keen interest in her market-basket, which she carried on her arm, and in a very few moments she became garrulous about her shopping experiences, displaying a pretty pride in her purchases. They included, I remember, three dried herrings and a pound of pig's-fry. The herrings we had for our tea, and I have never enjoyed a meal more.

In the evening, during a long walk through mean streets, Bellingham came to the point. He had said, you will remember, that he needed my help. What he wanted was no less than that I should play the part of conscience to him. I was to be instated, apparently, as his spiritual pastor. For the sake of that poor child happily darning his socks at home, I could not refuse the embarrassing honour thrust upon me. And when I learned that repentance was actually beginning to gain the upper hand of him I was glad, indeed, to exert any influence I possessed on the side of humanity. He had had a vile dream, he told me, and it was evident that he regarded it as a warning sent by that vigilant deity of his. In the dream his landlady, who believed him to be a legally married man, came and smiled at him over the bedrail, and wagged her head till it detached itself from the body and multiplied. The air was full of these grinning heads, poised like dragon-flies, all their evil eyes on Bellingham. Terror, he told me, took concrete form inside his own head : he could hear it simmering, sizzling, gurgling, boiling, splitting ; it drove him out of bed, away from Joan, and across the arid plains of hell under a sky monotonously grey except where the sun, a bloody red, like a huge socket from which the eye had been torn, stared sightlessly at him. Even as he gazed at it it filled and became menacing with the eye of God.

"It was a vision of hell," Bellingham said, wiping the moisture from his brow. "And the eye of God was even there. O Lord, how can I escape from Thy presence!"

It did not seem to me a moment propitious for argument, so I held my peace. He talked on about his doubts and his difficulties, his sin and his repentance; and at last I gathered that I was being invited to tell him whether he should stay with Joan or leave her.

"Oh, fling her into the streets," I advised him, with furious irony, "as her husband did."

"Yes," he said, mildly enough. "You're right. Against all my religious convictions I feel you to be right. I have made her my wife, and I must be faithful to my choice, right or wrong."

"It's as plain as day," I assured him. "Love and duty are pointing in the same direction for once. Why should you doubt it?"

"You see, Saunders," said Bellingham, with sudden fire, "it's all or nothing. She must remain my wife, or we must separate. There's no third way. I can't spend the rest of my life in the waters of Tantalus. I'm only a man, God help me!"

For a while we left it at that.

III

Saunders has an exasperating habit of stopping in the middle of a story, and behaving as though it were finished. He did this now. I reminded him that I was still listening. . . . No, I haven't done yet, he admitted. I thought that was the end, but it was only the beginning of poor Bellingham's troubles. You must imagine me now as popping in and out of his home pretty often. Those two remote rooms, like a fantastic nest built among London chimney-pots, attracted me by the romance they symbolized, by their air of being an idyllic peasant cottage, exquisitely clean, stuck away in the heart of the metropolis. Bellingham sent another urgent summons to me. It was the first of a series of alarms. The haunting began. The dreams that, every few nights, made Bellingham's sleep a thing of terror began now to invade his waking life. The Watching Eye was upon him, the eye of God, he declared it to be, trying to subdue him to submission. He heard a voice that said to him, " Put the woman from you." In short, he exhibited all the signs of incipient madness. At the time I thought it was indeed madness which threatened him. With one of his frantic telegrams in my hand—" I have seen God " or " He is come again in judgment "—what else could I think ? Yet I still believed that together he and I, with the courageous co-operation of Joan herself, might fend off the danger. She, poor girl, was tearful, but invincibly staunch. She would have sacrificed herself utterly for him, whom she loved with an unshakable devotion ; but I persuaded her that her going away, as she suggested, would not ease the situation. You will think me fanciful, no doubt, but sometimes I felt that Bellingham was fighting for his soul against some usurping demon, and that anything—death or damnation —was better than base surrender. And Bellingham, though he took a very different view of the nature of the contest, came to agree with my conclusion. He rejected my proposition but embraced the corollary. He conceived himself fighting against impossible odds, with no less than God, the Might and Majesty of the universe, as his implacable antagonist. " I tell you, Saunders," he said to me, " I saw Him plainly. He stood over there by my desk. He has incarnated Himself once more in order to crush my revolt." I passed over the almost maniacal egoism of the conception, and asked for a description of the Divine Visitor. " His body was all in strong shadow," Bellingham answered, shuddering at the recollection. " Only His terrible eyes were visible, and His accusing finger that pointed at me."

I had respected Bellingham ever since I had come to know him ; and now, if I respected his intelligence less, I felt something more than admiration for the indomitable spirit of the man. His unshaken belief that he was defying his Creator made fidelity to Joan a piece of titanic courage. Beset by horrors unspeakable, conscious that the citadel of his very reason was being stormed, he yet held doggedly to his determination. Doggedly at first, and afterwards with a sublime pride that I could not witness without an answering pride, a flaming exultation in the splendour of the human soul. Maniac or not, he extorted willing homage from me. You may say what you like about hallucination and the rest of it, but I tell you that to me, an eyewitness, the battle was lifted into the realm of cosmic drama where everything takes on a significance past mortal understanding but not past mortal apprehension. I thought of Job; I thought of Prometheus; and I thought of Bellingham as no mean third, championing life against death, championing youth, beauty, and all frail humanity, against the cruel bogy of the mind that menaced them. It goes without saying that his terrors derived all their power from his belief in their reality. He was blind to the plain facts of real religion, deaf to my rationalizing explanations of the horror that haunted him, obstinate in his conviction that God, and none other, was the author and agent of his persecution. Equally convinced was he that he had but to cast Joan out and he would save his soul alive. Every week saw a change in his physical condition. That brief period of his second blooming, fostered by the sweet presence and the maternal care of Joan, seemed over for ever; it was as if the seven years of spiritual famine were now to follow. He grew more gaunt, more haggard; vitality shrunk into him like a pent prisoner and peered out through those fiery orbs, his eyes, as through the mean windows of a condemned cell. He was locked fast in an impregnable isolation, from which no one could rescue him, it seemed, certainly not I, either by force or guile. He distrusted his food; he distrusted the men and women who passed him in the street. There were only two human souls he did not distrust: Joan herself was one, and I, by the mercy of heaven, was the other. He began to see a vast and sinister significance in all sorts of trivial events, all sorts of minor disasters that did not in the least concern any one of us, seeing in them the beginning of a cosmic disintegration that should engulf him in perdition. He was afraid yet defiant of these fatalities. He was both egomaniacal and illogical in his conviction that God, his implacable adversary, would behave like the veriest villain of melodrama rather than let him escape: tear the universe to tatters in order to compass the death or the dishonour of this one rebellious spirit, like a man who should pull his own house about his ears in the pursuit of a solitary rat. I myself began to scan the papers anxiously for wars and rumours of wars. Different as were our intellectual convictions, there was the stark comradeship between us of those who face death together. He watched for signs of God; Joan and I, with equal vigilance, watched him. And the stronger grew my affection for Bellingham, the shakier my own nerves became. Finally, with a kind of exultation, I threw up all my work—I was a curate at the time—and flung myself body and soul into this holy war. I found lodgings near Bellingham's, and visited him every day without fail. I felt that this fretting, this piling of horror upon horror, could not go on much longer. Sooner or later there would be a crisis; the increasing tension would snap. Mingled with my fear for Bellingham's sanity was a fear for the safety of Joan, caged up with a maniac. For a week or more we worried and waited.

IV

The end came with a sudden and sickening rush. And yet it was an end worth waiting and working for. In the street just outside his home, Bellingham was knocked down by a passing cab. Joan saw the accident from the window. By the sheerest chance he escaped with nothing worse than bruises and flesh wounds, but his excitement and terror reached their climax as he was helped back, limp and bleeding, to his rooms. The policeman, with a kindly word, handed him over to Joan's care. She was all for summoning a doctor, but Bellingham would not hear of it. White-faced, hiding his rising tumult behind a mask of steely calm, he told her curtly to fetch me. She obeyed, poor child, in terror of her life and his own. I was with them ten minutes later.

" Saunders," he greeted me, without preamble. " God has flung down His last challenge."

" You mean this accident ! " said I, scoffing gently.

" Accident ! " retorted Bellingham. " Do you, a priest of God, talk to me of accident ! Not a sparrow falls without God. No, it was no accident. It was the last warning. I feel in my bones that this is the end. At any moment now He will strike, and I shall burn in hell for ever more, where their worm dieth not and the fire is not quenched." He had the true missioner's flow of quotations, mostly misapplied ; but I knew better than to cross him then. Something of his own passion infected me.

We were standing in the bedroom, where he was at last submitting, with the most complete indifference, to the medical ministrations of Joan. " Let's go into the other room," I suggested, " and discuss this quietly and in comfort." I led the way, and they followed. The living-room, as I fancy they called it, was more cheerful by a long way. There was a fire in the grate, and a lamp like a great harvest moon glowed yellow on the table.

" Listen to me, Saunders," cried Bellingham, refusing to sit down. " You are my best friend, my only friend ; and Joan is my wife, the finest wife that any man had. The All-Seeing Eye is watching me now, as always ; that street-accident, as you call it, was the plain speech of God telling me to desert this woman. I'm a doomed man, Saunders, and I can speak my mind now. I believe in God as firmly as ever I believed in Him, but I have learned something. He is not worth serving. I tell you, Saunders, that the God we have both worshipped is as evil as He is powerful. Almighty Evil sits upon the throne of the universe, and I will curse Him and die." Poor fellow, he could not believe me when I told him that it was the God in himself that was speaking those wild words, the God in himself that was fighting a heroic battle against the demon of fear that Joan by her woman's tenderness had cast out.

There came, suddenly, a crash of something falling in one of the lower rooms of the house. It jarred our tense nerves horribly. And then, for the last time, the terror came to Bellingham, as if in answer to his taunt. He alone saw it, and you will quickly interpose that it was his mind alone that created it. And in a sense I believe you are right, but you'll find it hard before I finish to maintain that the apparition was a purely subjective thing. Can an hallucination cause windows to rattle and doors to move? I believe for my part that in some unfathomable way the old Bellingham, or rather the riot of evil fancies about God that had victimized the old Bellingham, had woven for itself some external form. Language is crude and clumsy, crushing the truth at which it grasps; but it seems to me that in some sense—and a sense not too metaphorical—the man was, as I said before, cloven in twain, divided against himself. But your face warns me that I'm boring you.

"There it is," shouted Bellingham, pointing towards a corner of the room. Joan, afraid of her lover, rushed to me, and my arms closed round her instinctively. We stared and saw nothing. "The same evil eyes," said Bellingham, more quietly, "the same accusing finger." And then began an uncanny one-sided colloquy. Bellingham conversed with his invisible mentor. "I will not leave her, God," said Bellingham. "I despise your dirty counsels. Kill me, damn me, burn me. Send me to hell, where I may see your hateful staring face no more."

The windows began unaccountably to rattle. Joan clung to me, sobbing, on the verge of hysteria. Bellingham strode towards the table and with one swift gesture put out the light. "I am not afraid of your darkness," he flung out.

For a moment, silence; and a darkness made ghastly by bright moonlight. Then the windows rattled again, and then, quite without warning, Bellingham collapsed and fell against me. My body had broken his fall, and I now released Joan in order to turn my attention to her lover. The sight of him prostrate restored her to courage. She was always ready when needed. I left Bellingham to her care for a moment and turned again to that haunted corner. I have never known fear such as I knew at that moment, and yet I felt infinitely braced by the dramatic significance of this conflict with an unknown terror. It was as if hell had invaded earth, and that God had left me as His sole witness. At such crises a man with religion turns to it. Your old-fashioned agnosticism will be shocked by my method of exorcising evil.

" In the Name of God the Father, God the Son, and God the Holy Ghost, I charge you to leave this man in peace ! " I made the sign of the cross.

And still I stared, and still I saw nothing. Joan was busy with Bellingham, who was beginning to show signs of returning consciousness. I could not move my eyes away from the corner by the door. And while I stared, something at last happened. Thank Heaven that I alone saw it ! The door leading to the bedroom, which had been left half-open, began closing. It closed, pulled to from the other side, and the knob moved and the catch clicked, as though released from the hand of the Unseen. I ran to it, opened it, and looked out. And saw—nothing at all.

From " The Street of the Eye "